NICHOLAS LICAUSI

THE LEADERS AND THE SPACE PROJECT

Inks and Bindings
888-290-5218
www.inksandbindings.com
orders@inksandbindings.com

CONTENTS

Foreword

I republished my first book "The Medical Project", and finished my second book, "Self Help and Mental Health, a Tough Path to Wellness (Our Story)" with my son collaborating with me. It is RECOMMENDED by US Review of Books.

Since these books were well received by many, I decided to keep writing and I completed my third book entitled, "The US Leadership Project", a fictional story taking on many different problems around the World. The US Leadership Program book was rated number 1 in Amazon. It's fascinating enough for me to proceed with, this book, a sequel, "The Leaders and the Space Project."

I wrote my first book right after my daughter's death. She would be alive today, if the medical industry would have been changed as we described in that book. In fact, millions of people would not have died if we would make better use of our technology as we describe in "The Medical Project" book.

It is an interesting fiction book presenting two heroes, John and Kate Colombo who work for the Government who tried their very best to improve the medical industry, however, there are also people who tried to stop them.

The couple are trying to build a medical computer that helps patients and doctors determine the best treatment for any types of disease or illness, and where to find the treatment.

After the book was completed, I called up senators and other government officials encouraging them to build this machine or computer, a breakthrough to the medical industry. However, they don't see the perspective beneficial from their end for financial reasons, or for any other reasons they only knew.

Today, there are few universities who are starting to implement the perspective presented in the first book, and hopefully they will be able to get enough funding to complete the project. Had this medical computer existed before the COVID virus started to spread, we wouldn't have to experience a terrible pandemic.

A screen play, a book trailer and an audio book has been made solely intended for the first book, "The Medical Project" because they could be vital elements in transforming the words into a movie.

On the other hand, the second book, "Self Help and Mental Health a Tough Path to Wellness (our story) which I wrote with my son based on his condition and he was motivated to work with me so he could give voice to his own mental illness, how it affects him and our family. We navigated on facts, personal challenges about mental health and other illnesses.

This book has received good reviews and ratings and in fact has garnered a whopping 4.8 stars out of 5 by Literary Agents and enthusiasts. Also, it was RECOMMENDED by the US Review of Books. They generally believed it should be in book stores close to schools and Universities so book readers would be informed and made aware of the mistakes we made as described in the book.

The Medical Project and Self Help and Mental Health a Tough Path to Wellness (our story)books were both in the NY Times Magazine.

This book evolved on John and Kate Colombo as main heroes in saving the world through the creation of the Medical Computer. Together, John and Kate became renowned through their lifesaving projects and truly, have saved many lives across different places.

I used to work with several big companies in the country and in my experience, I've seen the growth of each of these businesses by way of implementing innovative projects creating business processes that are profitable and favorable to the company. We should have these types of programs within and outside the US Government, all the more should be commissioned by the US government.

John and Kate are destined to be the faces of this program as described in my book, because they both have inventive minds. They have presented several patents of the projects and was able to acquire the approval of the government, mainly because of great benefits and impact to the American society. Until the projects are getting bigger and the impact is getting greater. Thus, in my 3rdbook, they were commissioned by the government to lead "The US Leadership Program" and they are highly regarded as high-ranking individuals and citizens.

The book talks about how the US Leadership Program got formed up and started with the aim to make the world a better place. And because its fiction, I've added the essential elements of some characters trying to kill and steal the secrets and information of the projects that John and Kate Colombo are working. The presentation of some realistic projects mentioned in the book are worth nothing for, as these projects are also timely for the current generation and the current world issues.

After my wife's death, I hardly survive every sunset because of my loneliness of missing her. We were in love from the time she was 17 and I was 19. I remember the Friday and Saturday nights when we went out. I still remember her. She was the total package. She was smart and beautiful. The writing helps me a lot. That is why I started writing this book which is my fourth book entitled, "The Leaders and the Space Project."

I have traveled around the world and have seen real scenarios happening in places that I have been, which made it easier for me to describe in my first, third and fourth books as I fictionalized the things and scenes happening at locations I used to work and live.

In matters of the heart, I know deeply as well what it feels like to be in love. I was in love with my wife for over 60 years. She was in high school then, and I was in my first year of college when we first met. She was so beautiful that I encouraged her to join the Miss Universe pageant, but she didn't agree.

In my three books, the love story between John and Kate Colombo is my love story reflection, where love and saving the world goes hand in hand.

I am an Aerospace Engineer, so I guess, that is where I got my problem-solving idea and present it in the book as my main characters' asset. Engineers love to solve problems and are mainly challenged by every bit of it. Solving and preventing problems from happening is not everyone's cup of tea. My books are full of problems that needed to be solved, thus, making John and Kate busy in solving the problems and saving the world. And because they have done so after series of projects, they become the targets that needed to be eliminated.

Now, high-profiled people have attacked them and tried to steal the secrets to solving the projects or stop them from implementing them, otherwise, these high-profiled individuals would financially bleed out.

In "The Medical Project" book, John and Kate Colombo are like Harrison Ford and Sandra Bullock. The very problem that they needed to solve in the book was to find the person that is responsible in stopping the medical project before he kills them and the rest of the people working on the project.

All of my books' main theme is about how we can improve the World and make life better for everyone. John and Kate have introduced a new technology that could potentially save the world today.

Other projects that John and Kate were working on were the Storm, Climate, Earthquake, Space and World Peace. Each of these projects have its own project leader representing the US and other countries around the World. All of these projects are described in full detail in my previous books.

The Storm project focuses on stopping hurricanes or typhoons by simply dispersing them off.

The Climate project, is to accumulate carbon or bad air and turned them into oxygen. The Earthquake project, is to predict where and when the next earthquake would occur and take actions ahead to save everyone just right before it happens. The Space project, is to build space stations in space using magnets and once a new propulsion system is developed traveling to Mars and other places in space would be possible. The World Peace project on the other hand, is to take rockets with nuclear warheads out in the air and relocate them in a safe place to be diffused and destroyed.

In the fourth book, the one I am writing now "The Leaders and the Space Project," John and Kate are completely respected and loved by the entire world and their leadership programs were duplicated in many major countries and the leaders in each country should report to John and Kate. Space travel will be the central theme of this book along with many other things that are realistically happening along the way.

John and Kate have greatly influenced other countries' perspectives about US, which could lead to world peace as they don't want to go against the US's plans and projects, as they all want to become partners in saving the entire humanity.

John and Kate have done so much for these countries and are happy to see their people enjoying life longer, and the overall improvement of their lives, they all owe it to John and Kate's inventiveness. So, John and Kate set off to find new ideas not just for the US but, this time, the mission is for the world.

My son has helped me with so many ideas to put in these books. We are hoping that someday, someone with money or even the government will build some of the things that we have described in these 4 books and implement them for the world's welfare.

You will see throughout this book that there will always be people who will try to steal some of the plans and ideas of John and Kate. This isn't just a love story between John and Kate, but it's a love story about loving the world we live in and saving the world before it's too late.

This book is one of the series of books that is written as fiction, but has a realistic feel with the problems our world is facing today and in the future. It presented various ways of improving our health around the world through technology, and how technology can help us solve the major problems of the World.

I deeply hope that this will reach many people and that somehow at least, read by someone with power that could make use of the ideas presented in this book, and get the projects started.

The world is waiting to be saved, we just don't know how much time we have before everything is too late.

The Terrorist Attack

John, Kate, and Katelin woke up in a new house which was in a large compound with twenty, 4000 square foot houses, where the President had put Kate, John, and their daughter Katelin in one of those houses to keep them safe from anyone trying to break into their house.

A Compound was built for the people who work for the government, and who have experienced attempts on their lives. John just woke up and looked like Harrison Ford when he got upset. He was very upset because he almost lost the 2 most important people of his life due to a terrorist attack. They were after the information that John and Kate had on various projects they were running.

Kate, who looked like Sandra Bullock, when she woke up was not as upset, but just thankful that both her husband and daughter were still alive. Their daughter who looked like a young Sandra Bullock in her 30's was just hugging her mom when they all woke up. Katelin has just recovered from an attempt on her life, when she was on her way to meet her parents for lunch. Though it was a couple of months ago, but then another attempt on their lives happened again. Good thing that they all moved into the compound now. They all feel relieved and safe.

John, Kate, and Katellin, were reviewing everything that happened with the FBI agent. They all went out but Kate and Katelin came home first and were taken hostage by the terrorists and when John came to the door, they had a gun pointed at Katelin's head and another on

Kate's head.

John asked what they wanted and they said they want to get the plans for the project. John instructed them that they needed to go to another room where the safe was so can get them.

When they did, while the guard was distracted John sneaked the gun out of the safe and put it in his pants covered by his shirt. He handed them the plans and they went back to where Kate and Katelin were. John knew the terrorists were going to kill them since they could identify who they were.

John had taught Kate and Katelin, some phrase codes which he also learned from his friend Bill, who graduated from West Point, and was physically fit working as a security guard for their projects. The phrase signal was if he said, 'please don't hurt my family' then Kate and Katelin would drop to the floor.

When John gave the signal, both Kate and Katelin dropped to the floor and John pulled out the gun and shot the 3 terrorists that were holding Kate and Katelin.

The FBI Agent said, "This all happened the night before and they move you into this new house across the street." John, Kate and Katellin all gave the FBI Agent a yes reply and the interview ended.

The plan was to move other government people that needed protection, into the compound. They are also going to increase security and put other leaders working closely with John and Kate in the same compound.

Jim, the President's Chief of Staff who looked like James Earl Jones, was upset about these attempts on their lives. Jim was discussing with the head of security how they could prevent it from happening ever again.

Jim and his wife Nancy, have known John and Kate for several years and used to go out together. Nancy was a beautiful African-American lady that used to be John's manager before she left the government, and started working for a consulting firm. She always sent John and Kate the most beautiful cards saying they were her best friends. Kate respected Nancy because she was so intelligent, with a master's degree from MIT on her belt.

The main objective of the terrorists was to get information on the projects John and Kate were working on, and then transmit it to their leaders so they could sell it or use it to start a war. The attempt by the terrorist failed mostly due to John, Kate, and several of the security staff. There were security guards who were killed or badly injured to protect John, Kate, and Katelin just to stop the terrorists from stealing information about the projects.

John, Kate, and Katelin did not get much sleep the night before. It was a cold and clear Monday morning in Washington D.C. They could see their old house which was just right across the street at the end of the block when the terrorist attacked them. There were about 20 federal agents investigating what happened. One could still smell the tear gas and see all the windows busted. The house was totally destroyed inside with the tear gas rockets in the wall. Also, the clothing and some of the computers have been destroyed and all the furniture were all destroyed as well.

John and Kate decided that they have enough exercise that makes them fit to fight off the people that broke into their house so they decided not to run this morning.

Katelin, called her bosses and told them that she will take the day off. Her bosses knew what happened as they all have watched it on TV.

John went to the door to ask one of the security guards why there's tear gas in the whole house. The security guard said that there are still some terrorists that are alive in the house after they all left and they would not come out so they have used a tear gas to drag them out.

John asked if they were clear to go to the house to see if they could find some things they could wear. The officer warned John the whole house smells tear gas and would just have to wait until they could clear the air and change all the air-conditioning filters so the smell would be completely gone. The guard did not clear John to go. He instead advised John to get new things to wear as their old stuff may not be safe anymore to use.

When John heard about the guard's recommendation, he knew Kate and Katelin would be happy to shop and get a whole new set of clothes and personal things. John also told Kate that they needed to talk to Jim and find out if he has any ideas who could be behind the attempt. They called Jim on the phone and said, "Hey there Jim, before we run off to pick up new set of clothes, we just want to know if you have any idea who's behind the attempt? "

Jim uttered in a tired but serious tone," Well, it was the construction people that were building, houses in the compound were infiltrated by the bad guys. The bad guys killed some of the security people guarding your house. That's why they were able to attack Kate and Katelin when they came home. We're lucky that nothing worst happened and that you were able to save Kate and Katelin with the phrase code which signaled them to drop to the floor and your quick action to kill the terrorist."

Jim continued, "I have put Bill in charge of the compound and he recruited new security people in place to make sure this never happens again in the compound. We were also able to capture few of them alive and we are questioning them now. I am also concerned about the contractors and universities we are using to build our systems. Anyone that works on these projects must have top secret clearance. I will make sure that Bill includes this in all of his security audits."

John responded in an appreciative tone and said, "Bill is good and we feel safe knowing he is in charge in watching over things in the compound. We will not be at work today because we need to replace some items. Everything in the house we were living in was destroyed. We will see you tomorrow and will do a complete review of all the projects."

Jim said, "Thanks guys. See you on tomorrow."

It was a beautiful day in Washington D.C. so Kate, John and Katelin changed their mind about their routine exercise and decided to go for a run in the compound instead, told the security team they would need to go to their old house and pick up some things and then go to the mall to do some shopping.

Kate called Valerie to set up a meeting for tomorrow with all the teams by 9 o' clock.

Katelin did the same thing too with her secretary. Tomorrow, Tuesday will be a very busy for the three of them.

Back to Work

John, Kate, and Katelin all woke up early and were eager to do their exercise and then get back to work. When John opened the door, Bill was standing there with a smile on his face and said, "Ready to exercise?"

John just smiled and said," Good morning, Bill. I heard you are now in charge of running the compound but I did not realize you would be running with us today. Kate and Katelin will be joining me, take a run to the gym, have breakfast, and then back here."

Bill responded with a smile and said, "I heard they put a diner there. It will be fun. I will be here waiting when all of you are ready."

When John got back into the house, he saw Kate dressed and he told the ladies, "Bill is going to join us in our run to the diner and have breakfast and then run back with us back here." Hurry up Katelin. Bill is waiting for us and will join us at the gym diner."

"I am ready when you are," Katelin hollered back at her parents.

As they were running around the compound, they could see that the security had greatly improved. There were guards all around the wall of the compound. Everyone working in the compound has a visible badge so they can be easily identified.

When John and Kate got to the restaurant, they asked Bill to sit with them as several other guards were posted inside and outside the diner. Bill mentioned that all the houses in the compound have to be completed in one month and all the construction people working on the housing project must be approved by his security team.

Everyone that gets in and out of the compound in the morning to do work will be thoroughly accounted for and the same procedure will be applied when they leave by 5 o'clock.

They are also instructed to let the security know where they will be at all times.

Bill enumerated to John and Kate the security procedures they are doing in each house, including frequent checking on the alarm system and increasing its volume if someone tried to break in again, elaborating that his security team will have a response time of 1 minute during break-ins.

After the security discussion during breakfast, John and Kate felt very safe. John is supposed to discuss security with Jim but after talking to Bill, he figured Jim has figured out the problem after what happened a couple of days ago.

John and Kate got to the office and conducted a briefing with the Medical, Storm, Climate, Earthquake, Space, and World Peace project leaders and asked each of them if they wanted to move into the compound. They all agreed that it is better than where they are right now, as they feel the compound is a much safer place. The majority of them have to discuss it with their family and come back tomorrow with an answer.

When John and Kate were all done with their meeting, they went over to Jim's office and Kate said with a very serious tone, "We were able to meet with Bill today and he seems to have everything under control. How are you doing Jim? You look a little tired."

Jim responded with a tired voice saying," The terrorist attack was bad for your family and until we stop these attacks, we will not be able to have enough sleep. Most of the terrorists were killed and the ones we captured alive are now being questioned by Jean Meadows so we can prosecute all the guilty parties. Four of our guards were killed and few are injured. The people responsible for this will get the death penalty and some of them will be spending many years in prison."

John then looked at Jim and said," Like Kate said, Bill is off to a good start. I believe Jean Meadows knows how to ensure these people will not attack us and others will think twice before they try anything like that again. We have asked the other leaders to stay in the compound since their lives will be in danger too, if they will be known to be working with us and are leading one of the projects."

"Let me know when we need to get them into the compound and we will make it happen. We have 20 houses built and ready to have 20 families move in if needed," Jim responded.

John smiled, "We are looking at using five houses as of the moment. One for each of the project leader with all the five projects we are currently working on."

Kate then raised her arm and said," We have not discussed this yet but Jean Meadows knows a lot about multiple projects and is also making enemies doing all these prosecutions so we need to talk with her and see if she feels at risk as well. Let's not forget Bill since he is the head of the compound security, his family needs to be protected too since he will be spending day and night ensuring all of our safety."

John and Jim agreed. So, it's something John and Kate would get back to Jim with a final decision from leaders including Bill and Jean.

Kate then said, "We will have Valerie set up a meeting with all the leaders, along with Bill and Jean tomorrow and we can meet up with you Jim after those meetings."

They left Jim's office. Kate immediately called Valerie and had her set up all the meetings including Bill and Jean while they headed their way back to the compound. Kate instructed Valerie to get their answer as soon as possible.

The couple arrived at their house. They looked around and saw that this was the first time they were alone in their house. What followed is a passionate moment, after all the scary things that have happened in their lives, they feel that they deserve to express their love to one another in the most intimate way they know how.

After the steamy act, John made dinner for both of them and they had a great time just talking about things other than the projects.

John and Kate knew each other from way back to their high school and college days. They were both very successful. Kate used to use the joke that if John died, he would marry a younger person. Contrary to the joke, they told each other they would only remarry if they were lucky enough to find someone they could love as much as they love each other. They would rather spend and enjoy their solitude rather than complicate their lives in meeting other people.

They then decided to go to bed early, watch Blue Bloods and for the first time they both got eight hours of uninterrupted sleep.

The Meeting

John and Kate woke up at around 6 o'clock and got ready for their daily routine exercise.

When John popped his head out the door Bill was right there and greeted him good morning with a smile. "I will be running with you guys today and there will be a couple of security people ahead of us and behind us."

John responded and said," That is good Bill, thank you. Oh yeah by the way Kate and I wanted to talk to you and see if you and your family will be interested in moving here in the compound."

Bill was a bit surprised but responded with a smile," The short answer is yes! We can talk more about it during our run. I will be here when you and Kate are ready."

John went back into the house and told Kate the good news about Bill. Kate was excited and said, "That's good to know. I believe that it is the best decision for him and his family."

During the run, Bill said, "This is why many people like working on your projects and with the both of you because you are always thinking of the welfare of the people and their families working with you on your projects. You also ask them about their problems and help them as much as you can. I believe that your projects help build a better world, a better place for everyone."

Kate felt proud of what Bill just said, "Thank you, Bill, that's just sweet to hear. We also believe, that you are not going to move your family here if it wasn't the safest place on Earth. You just tell Jim what you need to make this place very secure and he will make sure you get it. This compound will contain the Leaders of the most important projects the Government is working on. We need to keep them safe and secure while we're all working to build a better world."

Bill was truly happy that they have included him and his family to live safely in the compound. "This is not only something that will make my job easier, but it is something that I believe my kids will benefit from by being around such great people with great minds. Right now, we live in a good neighborhood and I can tell how our neighboring parents talk to their kids and even ours. As parents, we tend to influence what they will do next but somehow others can also take part of that influence, other factors that are not within our control, like, other parents, their friends and the environment."

The three of them were still running when John says, "Come on Bill, you graduated from one of our service academies. You are way above average. We are proud to have you on our team and you have kept us safe."

When they arrived at the gym, they turned on the sauna so it would be warm up when they completed the next two miles. When they got back to the sauna it was hot and they did some hot yoga in the sauna. After more than 2 hours, they were all done, had completed the routine, and were heading back home. John and Kate would always say, the hard part is over, now we get to refuel, which means she could eat and drink anything they want.

They ate breakfast, got dressed for work and then got in the limo that would take them to the West Wing to meet the Leaders.

Before the meeting, they discussed with Jim first their ideas about the expansion of the leadership team and also Jane Meadows' new job. Kate looked into Jim's office and said, "Do you have a few minutes for us to talk?"

Jim quickly called his secretary and instructed her to hold all incoming calls and other meetings until further notice from him. He then gives his attention to John and Kate who are both standing at his door and said with a serious tone, "I always have time for you both. What do you want to talk about?"

John spoke up first and said," We asked our leaders and also Bill and Jean to live with us in the compound for safety reasons. Bill gave us his positive response already. Now, since Jane Meadows is our overall project officer, she will be our second- in-command to whom project leaders will report to when we are unavailable. We would like to promote her to Project Leader with similar responsibilities as Kate and I have, but Jane would still report to us. That being said, she deserves to also have a salary increase. Apart from her project leader tasks she would still continue her prosecuting job. It is the job she is doing now without a title."

Jim said, "I like everything you said John, all of it. I will tell the President and the heads of the Congress and the Senate. I am sure they will approve but we have to wait until I get their ok's before you make the announcement to Jane. I will also give the Human Resources department a heads-up concerning this matter. I will get back to you both as soon as I get it all done," Jim gave them an authoritative look.

The couple are delighted to hear Jim doing the actions. Jim always understood where they are going with their suggestions and recommendations.

They then went to the conference room to meet and talk to each project leader, and Jean was put last on the schedule. The goal of the meeting is to convince them to live in the compound for their family's safety. They all wanted to move as soon as they could. That would give them extra protection for themselves and their families. It was also a mortgage payment that they will be freed from as the house designated to them will be free as long as remain as project leaders.

Jane had been coordinating with the bosses of the leaders around the world. John and Kate asked her to set up a meeting with them so they could let them know what the US was doing and encourage them to do the same thing.

Jean ran into some problems with some of the country leaders, so when she got back to John and Kate, she was disappointed but still is happy to announce.

"Almost all of the countries believe that what we are doing is right but they really would like to meet with you both sometime. Their country would like to get an update directly from you both on the status of the projects and where we will be going in the future with your new projects."

Kate then smiled and looked directly at Jean and said," Where do we stand on the terrorist that tried to steal our secrets and kill us? They did kill several security guards. I am asking this, because one of the main reasons why we are putting every leader and yourself in the Compound is because we are concerned that the same thing will happen to any of you, and it could happen to any country too. If this is just one group of people and we catch them all, that would be one thing, but if it is a bigger plot then all leaders would be in great danger. Can you give us an update on what you found out from the terrorists we captured alive."

Jean was exactly like Bridget Moynahan, in Blue Bloods, and that is why they hired her. She was so confident when she said, "I questioned all of them and let them know we could give them the death penalty because they killed government agents. A couple of them talked and said that they were hired by someone from the Iranian government and was given a lot of money. They don't have a name though."

John with his disappointed tone said," That means this could happen again. I believe the President and the rest of the world are doing what they can to isolate this concern. I guess we are hoping they will change their leaders. We need to meet directly with country leaders that has the potential to not implement similar projects that we have and hear them out and their reason for doing so. We do that either by phone or face-to- face meeting.

Jean added, "Three countries that are next on our list have shown to be potentially attacked and have not implemented the compound concept. The first one is Japan and they say it is very difficult for a terrorist to enter their country because of their VISA process. Then we have Mexico, England, and France as the next three countries whose cost of living is very expensive.

Kate then said with astern voice, "For these three countries that you are saying are too expensive, could you please find out if you can find the money for these countries that we could use to pay for their compound? For the Japan case see if there is a difference between our VISA process and theirs. Also, if you can find out how many attacks have happened in Japan."

Kate then turned to Natalie and said," tell Jim and Valerie that we are planning on using one of our Jets to fly to these countries, but first, see if they will allow us to do this on a Zoom call.

Let's meet tomorrow and talk about this and see if we can arrive at a unanimous decision. Also, Jean, I need to know your decision about your moving into the Compound."

With a smile, Jean said," Thank you for allowing me to move into the compound, by the way. Yes, I will do it. and you have made my mother very happy. She was worried about my safety. Now she can live stress-free."

John then turned to Jean in a serious tone," Would you and Natalie be fine if we sit down and set up a half-hour meeting with you to discuss the compound and some other items? Also, tell her to set up similar meetings individually with each of the leaders." Jean nodded.

It was 6 pm so John and Kate decided that they would go home early and work from home but decided to drop at Jim's office on the way. They found him not busy so Kate looked into his office and said, "Did you get the numbers back from HR about the salary increases and titles."

Jim said with a big smile, "Everything has been approved and if you come to my office in the morning, I will give you the details on each promoted individual."

John and Kate were very happy, went home to eat dinner, made love and went to bed early because tomorrow is going to be another big day. They fell asleep on the thought if there's any day that is not going to be a big day.

The Meeting with the Inventor

John and Kate woke up at 6 o'clock as usual without having to have the sound of any alarm waking them up. Both decided they would run up to the diner in the gym, have some breakfast, and run home. When John popped his head out the door Bill was already there, dressed for running, and said," Will you be running again with us today, John?"

It was still early and John was half awake but responded," Yes, of course, Bill. Kate and I will be running to the diner. We should be ready in about 30 minutes."

When John went back inside the house, he told Kate that Bill would be running with them to the diner and they should be ready in 30 minutes. Kate finished dressing up and got ready to run.

When they left, John asked Bill, "Did you already move into the compound?"

Bill responded with a positive tone," We moved in yesterday and that is why I was right at your door. I was checking on the security to make sure there's someone outside your house patrolling the area. There were two of them so I relieved one of them and the other is still at your house. This place is as secure as the White House. The terrorist problem we had a few days ago hopefully, will never happen again."

Kate put a smile on her face and said," We feel very safe with you around Bill. You saved our lives a few days ago when you taught John that trick about having us drop to the floor as soon as John says 'Please don't hurt my family', phrase code. We are grateful for you."

Bill then responded to Kate with a serious tone," It made me feel so good when John told me he used that trick. He has saved my life a few times too. We have each other's back all the time. I know you both have each other's back also."

They finished half of their run and walked into the gym and Kate said," Katelin, our daughter helped get this diner in our gym. I hope they are making money and everything is fine."

Two more security guards were running with them as they sat at a table near the door with a full view of the restaurant even though they were the only one there. John and Kate asked Bill to join them so he did. They talked more about doing security audits in each of the countries for the upcoming trip to England, France, Mexico and Japan.

They also let Bill know that the trip has not been finalized and they would have to meet with Jim for his approval. They ran back home with Bill and prepped for work. John could not take his eyes off of Kate when she's all dressed up and ready for work. She was just so beautiful in his eyes.

John did a quick reminiscing in his head during the times when they were dating. She's still the same Kate he knew, as beautiful as when he first saw her. Today, she still has the same physique and figure despite the demands from the work that they are doing. Almost every day she receives a compliment from someone about how she looked and carried herself. It's like she has not aged at all.

They were out the door hopped in the limo, and are heading to the West Wing. When they walked in, Jim waved them into his office. He told them to sit down and a big smile on his face means something good is happening.

"I was able to get the titles and increases in salary for all of your leaders including Jean who is now promoted as Project Office Leader."

John and Kate were so happy to hear the news that they immediately shook Jim's hand but Jim all of a sudden looked serious." Sit down because I have something else to tell you."

John and Kate looked surprised because he had given them everything they had asked for. So, they sat back down with a curious look on their faces.

Jim then smiled and said," I know both of you would not ask for this but everyone wanted to do something for both of you because you have done so much for the country and the world. I know that you would never ask for anything but the President and the head of Congress and Senate, all wanted to give you both an increase on your salaries and a pension when you both retire. By the way the other leaders will be getting a pension when they retire as well. I hope you and all the leaders will consider this from a very grateful nation. We're all grateful for your contributions."

When John and Kate walked out of Jim's office, they felt really happy. The happiest they have ever been and they walked into the conference room for their first meeting with Jean.

Kate signaled Jean to sit down and start with a very happy tone." I have some good news for you. You will be doing the same thing you have always been doing but now you will have a title as the Project Office Leader. Here's the sweetest part, you will be getting an increase in salary and a pension when you retire. The country and both of us appreciate everything you have done and everything you will do. Keep up the good work and enjoy the safety of the compound which the government will allow you to live in for free, as long as you have this job."

Jean then got up and hugged both John and Kate with tears in her eyes because of the joy she felt. Before she left, she told John and Kate that the initial arrangements were being made to visit England, France, Mexico, and Japan and that the leaders would want to meet with them before they could finalize the request. Other countries have also made such requests and changes to match the current plans of the US.

The next Leader to see them was already at the door so they waved him in and John said," Paul you have been on the Medical Project with us from the beginning. We met in college; you were best man at our wedding and we ended up reaching our goals. Me becoming an Engineer and you becoming a psychiatrist, of which you left your practice to help us build the Medical Project around the World. Now as the leader of the Medical Project around the world, I am proud and happy to tell you that, on behalf of the US government, you will receive an increase in your salary and a pension when you retire. Your title will be Leader of the Medical Project and as long as you are working with us, you will have the house in the compound to live in for free."

John congratulated Paul with complete sincerity. Paul became a bit emotional as he said," I have told you when you called me to work to start the Medical Project that it would be my joy and honor to work with you and it has been fantastic since then.

I have one concern though, because you know I do not want to do anything that would hurt you or Kate. You both know I am gay and now if I live in the compound other people may realize this and I do not want to get you in trouble."

Kate intervened in an upset tone," If anyone brings that up. They will be in a lot of trouble.

We and everyone above us have no problem with that and we have a great deal of power so you being gay is not a problem. So will you accept the new title and consider the salary increase because you deserve this. Also, from now on consider the Compound as your new home, and you don't have to worry about anything else, ok?"

Paul with a tear in his eye said," You know I will. You are the best friends I have and I want to support anything, you both are working on. The Medical Project has really changed the world and saved a lot of lives, so it is my honor to be the Leader of The Medical Project. I guess we will be seeing a lot more of each other since we are now in the same neighborhood," he said with a sheepish grin. Paul stood up and hugged John then Kate and left the room a very happy person.

The meetings with the Storm, Climate, Earthquake and World Peace leaders all went well and everyone agreed to move to the Compound, so it was a very successful day for the leadership team, especially for John and Kate. They felt that their mission for the day was accomplished.

When John and Kate went home, they gave Katelin a call and they all agreed to meet at Deanne's place in one hour for dinner. And there they each shared a great day story and a great dinner for the three of them as a family.

John and Kate needed to get to work at 9 o'clock tomorrow to see what trips were planned and confirmed for them. Jean was initially setting it up for them with the other leaders and would meet her first thing in morning.

They went to bed early so they could get in an early run. It was indeed another big day for them, literally, and a fantastic one.

Meeting with Jean Meadows

John and Kate woke up as usual at 6 o'clock without any alarm and did their morning routine run to the diner in the gym, have some breakfast, and off to work.

When John popped his head out the door, as usual, Bill was already there, dressed for running, and said with a more perky smile," Ready to run with you John when you are."

John laughed and said," I am sure glad you moved into the Compound, It makes it a lot easier for you, your family and us. We will be ready Bill, in about 15 minutes."

Kate was already dressed and she was putting on her shoes when John said," You look more beautiful every day. Oh, I told Bill we'll be out by the door in 15 minutes. I am sure a lot of residents in the compound are glad they put that diner in the Compound. I will check on Katelin and see if she wants to join us," giving his wife a wink.

John tapped on Katelin's door and then opened it slightly and noticed she was still fast asleep so he just didn't want to wake her. He went back and told Kate their daughter's morning status. Kate uttered," She doesn't get off that easy!"

She rushed to Katelin's room and was confident that she knew how to wake her daughter up and she started to tickle her with a whisper," How about some nice fresh brewed coffee and some potatoes and eggs."

Katelin rolled over and with her eyes half shut and a smile on her face she said, "We are running to the diner right. I know I need to do this because I have not exercised in over a week. Give me 15 minutes, Mom," while trying to open her eyes wider.

Kate knows that Katelin would always wake up with a smile since the day she was born and would not be upset even if she needed to wake her up. She went to the door and saw Bill there and said, "Katelin will be joining us so give us another 15 minutes. And Bill, you join us for breakfast when we get to the diner, alright?"

Bill nodded, he then turned to the security in charge next to him and said, "I want two guards to stay here at the house and the other two to go to the diner with us. Also, tell the limo driver that we will be ready to go to the West Wing around 8:30. If you see Katelin's limo driver you can tell him Katelin will be ready around 8:30 also."

Kate thanked Bill with her sweet smile for taking care of everything. Then she went back into the house and saw that John and Katelin were putting on their running shoes and socks and at the same time looking around for their caps. It's a sight to behold for Kate. Father and daughter moment.

How they move together. You could tell they were father and daughter. People use to tell John and Kate that she looked just like Kate. John and Kate always thought she looked more like John. She had the best of both of them. Kate enjoyed watching them for a moment.

It was a beautiful morning and John was thinking that he will always remember this very moment running up to the diner with these two VIP of his life. The runs and conversations when the three of them are together are always unforgettable. They would always sit across from each other and talk about any problem they were having, or listening to Willie Nelson and Toby Keith songs from the jukebox and then run home. Kate wanted to always sit across from John. She said it was what she always wanted so she could see his eyes when they talked. John always will remember these mornings. This morning. they were talking about the upcoming trips and what Jean may have to tell them when they get in the office later.

After they completed their breakfast and morning run, they were right on schedule and are already in the West Wing conference room at exactly 9 o'clock, and Jean was sitting there with some charts to present. Jean stood up and said," I really like you both because when you know you need to be some place, you are always on time or ahead of the time.

John responded with a smile," I guess it is something we learned when working as consultants and with our customers. You don't want to keep a customer waiting or anyone of importance for that matter. This is true in almost every country except Latin America."

And he shared an experience, "I remember one time, we were supposed to meet someone at a bar at 5pm in Mexico City. I was there a little before 5pm and then the person that worked for me and set up the meeting came in around 5:20pm. I asked him' what time are we supposed to meet?'. He told me '5 o'clock' and then he said that he's sorry for being late. Then I asked him where the other guy was, I only got a response of "I am sure he will be here shortly." He laughed when he remembered the experience.

John's employee then responded in a serious tone saying, "Don't expect him to say he is sorry for being late like I did. In Mexico or in many Latin American Countries you are not expected to be right on time. They will arrive whenever they want to, not being sorry for being late and carry on the meeting like he was right on time." That is what happened when the customer arrived.

"Also, I noticed when Kate and I were invited to a Latin America event where there are maybe about a hundred people and we were the only people there at the specified time and the others all showed up 30 minutes after the scheduled time."

Jean was always impressed with the experiences that John and Kate had, but she knew that it was exactly the reason why they were respected and listened to around the World.

They knew how to blend in with different cultures. She also knew that the couple was always teaching people who worked for them good values especially those who are willing to learn including her.

Jean went back to her thoughts and said," I have some good news and some bad news.

The good news is that when I went to Jim, he told me that the President approved of your travels using a government- issued plane. They were thinking with all the money we have saved in all of the projects; we should have a jet but until that is approved you need to use the one that is available for the meantime."

"Jim would not approve the trip unless you used an Air Force jet and a helicopter service to the Embassy in the countries that you'd be visiting. The bad news on the other hand, is that all the country leaders would want to personally meet both of you before they can make the necessary changes. And what makes it bad is that there's quite a lot to visit. I can just imagine the exhaustion of country hopping." Jean said with her not-so- happy face.

Kate retorted, "We could not reward countries that will not do what we would like them to do most especially if it's concerning their leader's safety. Those countries that are doing what we suggested, we don't need to even visit them, virtual meetings would do. We also need to know what countries have the best results on the Medical, Storm, Earthquake, Climate, Space and World Peace projects. We will visit those countries and also prioritize the visit to England, France, Japan and Mexico.

Jean immediately cut Kate off before she can say more, "I can give you that answer now since I keep a scorecard on my weekly reviews with the US Leaders and World Leaders. The US leads in every category but as for other countries; Russia leads in the Medical Project. China leads in the Storm Project. Japan leads in the Earthquake Project, and since Russia and China are the only ones that went into Space with us then they both lead in that category. The World Peace category only has the US implementing that so we have no one leading in that category other than the U.S."

John then said," That would mean we would add China and Russia to the original list. I like that list because China and Russia are both vital to making the Projects a success and that means they are doing their job, except for World Peace project."

Then he continued, "I would say to get the trip set up with the pilot that will be flying us to all these places, and please start setting up the meeting with the Leaders in those countries as well including their decision-makers."

Kate added the instructions, "Since we will have our jet you and all the other project leaders should be on this trip, which means they have to put someone in charge on their behalf when they are gone. If they don't have someone that would be the backup when they are gone, then they can't go because I do not want anything to get behind. When everything is set up, go to Jim and see if he, or the President, would want to join on any of these trips. Please use Natalie or Valerie to help you in making all of these arrangements."

Jean responded with a proud smile on her face and said, "This will be the trip of my lifetime. I can't believe I have the honor to be visiting all of these countries and meeting with all these high-level people. The leaders and I feel so blessed to be on this project."

With what Jean said, John remembered his big trip to Asia. Kate had a different job then.

So, he traveled alone and he was thinking the same as Jean at the moment. It was the trip of a lifetime to new people and new cultures in different countries.

Then John said, "I had to take Kate because I wanted to share that experience with her. I had the same feeling as you have Jean. I paid for her to come using my own money or frequent flier miles. It was a dangerous trip but you're right, it was the trip of a lifetime. In some countries, they suggested I fly in and out and not stay overnight. In other countries, they just would not let me go."

"I had this trip to Jakarta, Indonesia, but, because there were kidnappings and anti-American sentiment at that time. I was attending meetings during the day and Kate would just stay in the lobby of the hotel and visit as many gift shops as she can. I was so happy to see her when my business meetings were over and I bet she was even happier to see me too." as she teased his wife with his cute smirks.

"I told the executive I was meeting with in Jakarta, that I had to pick up my wife at a hotel and I am sure she would want to do some shopping. He looked at me with surprise and said, please take my driver and car he will take you to some places and then to the airport. I talked with the driver and found out he was not only a driver but also his bodyguard and was carrying a gun with him. He did take us to some nice places and Kate did get some things. We never discussed how we felt that day."

Kate and Jean were simply entertained by the way John shared his travel experiences and they both just listened to him when they sensed that there was no sign of John stopping from sharing his other trip-of-a-lifetime moments.

And he continued still, "Another one, when I was in Kuala Lumpur in Malaysia, I remember arriving at noon and the sun was so hot and then having to take a cab into the city but none of the cabs had air condition. And there I was in a three-piece suit sweating the whole time of my cab ride.

Rolling down the window did not even do any good since it was hotter outside than in the cab."

And then he realized he was talking for minutes, he then reverted to the current situation, which surprised Kate and Jean because they enjoyed his tell tales.

He then said, "I won't allow it to happen this time because we will have an Air Force jet to take us there and a helicopter to take us to the Embassy and we will likely be staying at the embassy in every country. I am not sure what will happen on this trip but I am sure there will be some excitement and a lot of work to do. I don't want to ruin the feelings of everybody so I won't tell them about all the things that happened on our last trip to Asia."

There was a lull in the conversation for a while and then Kate looked over at John and she said with a frantic loud voice, "John, is everything ok! It seems that you were in another world for a minute there."

John just smiled and said, "I am ok, just daydreaming. I told you when I was young, I was the kid in school, that looked out the window and was engaged in deep thought about something nice I was going to do after school, while the teacher was talking." Now, he couldn't stop thinking about the trips they had in the past and this upcoming one.

Then, he focused back at Jean, and said, "This will be a trip of a lifetime. Let's make sure there aren't any surprises along the way and we stay out of danger as much as possible."

Kate just looked over at John and knew what he meant and figured out that indeed he must have remembered those trips they had way back. Well, I'm confident that this one should be easier and safer since we will have our bodyguards traveling with us," she added. Then looked at Jean and said, "I guess we will need one more meeting to finalize the trip plans and for you to get approval from Jim concerning others joining us. Why don't we meet on Tuesday afternoon and that will give you a chance to meet and talk with all the people? As I said before get Valerie and Natalie to help you out with some of the logistics."

Jean agreed and heeded all the instructions given to her at once and concluded their meeting. It's already 6 pm, and John and Kate decided to stop by at Jim's office before heading home.

And just right on time Jim is also heading home himself so they talked the business for the day while they are walking out. They wished each other a great weekend and they parted ways.

When John and Kate got home, they noticed a message from Katelin telling them she's out on a date with her doctor friend that did the surgery to remove a bullet in her chest and she would not be home until late so don't wait up for her. John looked a little upset with the message but Kate was really happy so John was not worried at all.

John made dinner that night for both of them and they went to bed early.

The Weekend

John and Kate woke up at 8 am a bit later than usual, well it's the weekend. When they walked out their bedroom door, they noticed Katelin was waiting for them in her running clothes.

She put her hands on her hips and said with a big smile." I guess this is the latest you ever woke up.

I thought I was going to have to go in there and drag you out of bed so you could go for a run with me. We can all relax today. For you two it just means you can exercise more." with her energetic way of talking to them.

Katelin could always get a smile out of John and Kate. It's impossible for them as her parent not to smile or laugh when she tries to crack a joke. This brought back a memory of John.

"Katelin, I remember the time we were all sitting at the table having dinner and we started going around the table telling each other jokes we heard. You were a teenager by then, and it was your turn to tell a joke and so you thought for a minute and then said, *'How do you turn off a light switch?* We could not guess the right answer and then you said, *'With a peanut butter and jelly sandwich.* Then you started laughing at your joke. Even though it was not a good joke at all, we could not hold back seeing you laugh so we started laughing too," and we all started to laugh very hard. "It took us a few minutes to get over that and stopped laughing. I had to tell you it was not a real funny joke so you would not embarrass yourself by telling others that joke." That is when Kate and John realized that Katelin could make anyone laugh or cry by just looking at her face.

Kate with a big smile said," Well looks like we got a lot of catching up to do. A 2.5-hour exercise and then maybe we can go to the mall, do some shopping and see a movie. I believe Mission Impossible is playing. Give us 30 minutes and we will be ready to run."

Katelin with a naughty smile said," I'm in! I will let security know what we are going to do today. You guys' hurry cos you're so behind schedule," as turned away rolling her eyes.

Kate turned to John and said, "We are very lucky. The 3 of us are always trying to do things that would make us a family. Katelin knows the music we like to hear; she also knows where we like to go and she is always trying to make us happy and we are doing the same thing for her. So today is the day when we can relax with Katelin. So, let's get going," as she pushed her husband to prepare for their morning run.

The 3 of them completed their morning exercise and got dressed for shopping and a movie.

When they got to the mall it was too early to get lunch so they shopped for about a half hour and then went to the Cheese Cake Factory and got some lunch and then went to the movie. It was a relaxing day except when they were walking out of the movie to the limo, someone came running up to them yelling their names. As soon as they got within 5 feet from them a security guard jumped in front of them and blocked the man. He tried to break free of the security guard but the other guards brought him to the ground and then a gun popped out of his pocket. Then the guards pinned him to the ground put handcuffs on him and brought him to another car while John, Kate, and Katelin got into the limo.

John said with some disappointment, "I thought we were going to have one day where we could relax. I will give Jean a call when we get home and let her know what happened," while shaking his head with much disappointment. The ladies were just quite on their way home.

When they got home Katelin went to her room and made some

calls to her friends. John and Kate made a conference call to Jean and John asked her in a disappointed tone," Hi Jean sorry to spoil your weekend but it happened again. There is another person that may have his life interrupted for a while."

They then described the whole incident and Jean said," Sorry this keeps happening. I will dig into it and find out if he is just a fan or if he tried to do you both some harm. In either case, he will be sorry about what he did and will regret it. I will go and question this person now, and find out what his story is. I am happy that the security got him on time."

John and Kate then went to bed and turned on the television. They decided they would not do any work today but tomorrow they will start making plans for the upcoming trip. They didn't set the alarm because they wanted to get as much sleep as possible. Tomorrow they were thinking they would wake up and go straight to Church and then do their exercise and then do some work at home. Another day, another attempt on their lives. When will this end? It's the last thing that is floating on John's mind before he drifts off to sleep.

Church & Home

John and Kate woke up at 8 am which was two days in a row. Now where they slept late. They probably needed the rest. John looked at the Church's schedule for Sunday mass and noticed there is a mass at 10 o'clock so he opened the door and updated the security that they would be going to the Church at 9:30 and then coming home to exercise and do some work.

Kate went into Katelin's room woke her up and said they were going to the 10 am mass and were leaving at 9:30. The three of them are in their Sunday's best outfit, head their way to the Church. They arrived a little before 10 and when they walked in, they did notice that some people are looking at them and even pointing saying they were seen on TV a lot. Anyway John, Kate and Katelin attended the mass in peace. They found 3 seats together so they knelt down and each said a few prayers before the mass began.

When the Priest walked in and started the ceremony it seemed like he was looking straight at them the entire time. Then when it came time for the Priest to come to the pulpit to say a few words he acknowledges John and Kate by telling everyone in the Church everything they had done and also how dangerous it has been for them. He asked everyone to pray for them.

John and Kate, somehow get embarrassed when people complement them and but they just looked at the Priest and nodded their heads with a motion to thank him, when he was done. They then continued their prayer for health, wisdom, wealth and happiness for each other. They also prayed for people that they knew that are no longer with the living.

When they left mass, they were surrounded by security guards so no one could approach them because security knew after the Priest said all those things then everyone knew they were there and it would be a perfect time for anyone who has the agenda of killing them. When they got to the limo, Bill was waiting and told them they had to exit from Church the way he did to make sure they got out fine.

John, Kate and Katelin, knew that would always be at risk in the public. They thanked Bill for being on top of things. They decided to change things and made their way to Deanne's Place for lunch before going home. Bill radioed security for the changes ready and also to make sure it would be safe for them to have lunch at the location.

Every time the family dined at Deanne's Place it seemed it was a very safe place for them to enjoy a scrumptious meal. The place is named after the daughter of the owner who died, the mother told them that the place is protected and looked after from above by Deanne.

John and Kate asked Bill to sit at their table so they could talk about security and the upcoming trip. Katelin knew they were going to talk business so she asked one of her friends to join her for lunch and they moved to another table.

Kate apologized to Bill, "Sorry to make you work on a Sunday and take you away from your family but we need to discuss our upcoming trip because the discussion with the other countries involves a great deal of security. We are asking them to protect their leaders similar to what we have implemented in the compound."

Bill responded with a serious tone," My wife and I understand the importance of what you are doing and she's proud of me for working on this project with you and keeping you safe all the time. Now, it is just fair to do the same thing for all the leaders around the world to be safe."

John then said," For each country we will visit, we need to show them the cost of building the compound, why it is safer and less costly than protecting people in their own houses. We also need to show them how we save money by implementing all the projects we have to protect their Leaders."

Bill then responded by saying," I will have everything put together before the trips. I have to start making the preparations today."

John and Kate both smiled and Kate then said," Outstanding! Also, plan on doing a security audit in each of the countries we will visit. Here comes our lunch! We can talk more tomorrow with Jean at about 10 am and we can put everything together for each country before our trips, meantime let's enjoy our lunch."

While they were eating John called Valerie and gave her instructions to set up a meeting by 10 o'clock by tomorrow - Monday.

When lunch was done, they noticed Katelin and her friend had left already in Katelin's limo and security designated for her. She left a message though, saying she was going back to work for a couple of hours and then meet them at the house tonight at 8 o'clock.

When John and Kate read the message, they both looked at each other thinking the same thing. They were proud of their daughter and what she has become.

The Upcoming Trip

John and Kate woke up at 6 am from the alarm going off. They both got dressed for a run and Katelin met them in the living room all dressed in her running clothes and they all decided to run to the diner in the gym, have some breakfast, and run back home. There's so much to look forward to today.

As soon as they opened the door, they saw Bill all dressed in his running outfit and they all ran to the diner with four other guards. Two in front and two behind them. With Bill leading the security detail. The family felt very safe.

After they finished their breakfast and exercise, they were on their way to the West Wing and Katelin was on the way to her work as well and they carried on their day.

John and Kate went straight to Jim's office and gave him an update on their trip and asked if he and the President will be joining them on any of the trips. Jim mentioned he will probably go to some of the countries but depending on his schedule of availability.

They then proceeded to the conference room where she was waiting for them. Jean greeted them with a warm smile on her face and said, "I have very good news. Every country leader I was able to speak with, have all shown interest in meeting both of you."

With excitement she added, "So you will be meeting with the Prime Ministers in England and Japan. The Presidents in France, Mexico, Russia and China also agreed to meet with you."

"These countries understand what's at stake here and I believe that they will implement what you will be presenting to them as they also would want to achieve the same results that we have as a country."

Kate and John looked pleased from what she heard from Jean," We better have Bill play a major role on the trip and have him set up his own security team reporting to him just like what projects leaders report to us. He should lead this and cascade the similar procedure to the rest of the countries because the priority is to protect all project leaders and the same thing has to be done to countries who would like to follow us."

She then turned to Jean and instructed her to talk to Bill and informed him of his role in the upcoming trips.

"Please let Bill know our plans and also brief Natalie to prepare possible speeches from the President should he be joining in one of our trips and it has to be reviewed and approved by the office of the President, Senate and Congress. Lastly, make sure Valerie has all the necessary logistics, people and things that should not miss or be missed on these trips, and should there be meeting set with Jim and the President prior to the trip, let us know immediately."

Jean as if taking all the military command attentively take in all that Kate said, "I will set the meeting for tomorrow to discuss our trip itineraries in each country."

Kate and John had back-to-back meetings with their assistants to make sure all bases are covered.

It's been a long day full of meetings, preparations and so much anxiety on what lies ahead and what awaits them in their upcoming trips to other countries.

Then they went home feeling exhausted and both decided to cook for dinner and enjoy a peaceful dinner at home. They have tried waiting for Katelin to join them but they knew she must have buried herself with so much work just like them. She got her DNA from them that's for sure.

They went to bed and doze off not long after they have lied down.

The night was quiet and so they enjoyed an uninterrupted sleep once again.

The Arrangements

ohn and Kate always watched TV before going to bed. They got interested in Jack Ryan and they started watching it last night and were hooked to it until they realized they were up until 2 a.m. It is now a popular TV series about CIA operations. It's the only other thing they try to watch aside from Blue Bloods because they have seen most of the shows so at times when they get to sleep early the TV just keeps playing.

The next morning, they made sure they set the alarm so they could wake up on time since they were not able to sleep early. The alarm went off at 6 o'clock and they both woke up and ran to the diner, had breakfast, and then ran back home and got ready for work. They were at Jim's office at about 9 o'clock to discuss the trip but Jim was engaged in a different meeting with the President's cabinet members so they went straight to the conference room and Jean was already there together with Natalie and Valerie.

The ladies stood up when John and Kate walked in and Jean with a beaming smile," I believe we have the whole trip completely set up along with each country's itineraries. Your first stop will be England and you will meet and have dinner with the new King, the King's wife, Prince William, and his Royal Family. Then you will meet the Prime Minister and their key people. The next day you will be flying off to France."

John interrupted Jean and said in a serious tone," Why are we meeting with the Royal Family?"

Jean smiled and said," It is really due to the request of the royalty children. The kids had a discussion in their class about some great Americans and when their teacher found out you were visiting the Palace, they wanted to take the opportunity to meet you," proudly explained the reason.

John and Kate were so pleased upon hearing the story, and they felt a genuine joy in their hearts knowing they have made an impact even to children. Kate said with a smile," I think it would be great to meet with them and give them some kind of presents to show our appreciation, I'm sure the press would air it on TV."

Natalie excused politely," I hope you don't mind but my kids have to make something for their class about where I worked and they made this nice thing and got an A for doing it.

They had to show their class where I worked and they made two pictures which showed all our projects. One of Kate and one of John with all the projects on each of the photos and something about each project, it was very sweet."

John and Kate don't want to be superstars but John considered it a very good suggestion to show it to the teacher in England so John said jokingly," I guess it's ok since it is for kids and their teacher. Have a bunch of these made just in case we run into more kids on this trip." As she directed his instruction to Natalie.

Kate added," At least they got an "A". Let your kids know what we plan on doing with their idea and thank them for that. Let's make as many as they can."

Natalie felt so proud of her kids, and could not wait to get home and tell them the good news. She just smiled and said," Thank you both. I guess we are all proud to be working on these projects with both of you. I will have them start creating what they have done at school."

John and Kate just smiled back and nodded," John and I are so happy that you ladies are on this team. Together we can do greater things for the world."

Jean butted in, in the conversation," We are so proud to be a part of the team, your team.

Oh, before I forget, you will be staying at the U.S. Embassy in all of the countries. You're both scheduled to fly a day after tomorrow. So, you will be in England on Wednesday and Thursday, and France on Friday and Saturday. On Sunday you will fly to Moscow. You will spend three days in Moscow and then fly to Beijing on Thursday next week. Then, you will leave Beijing on Friday to proceed to Tokyo and leave Tokyo on Sunday. You will spend your Monday, Tuesday, and Wednesday in Mexico City. On Thursday you will fly back home. It will be two weeks of travel." she's gasping for breath reading all the schedules.

John and Kate approved the plan and told Jean and Natalie to set up meetings with all the leaders on Wednesday before the trip and prepare the necessary reports on the statuses of each of the projects. In addition, there will be a security audit in each country as soon as they arrive.

John and Kate are done for the day called their daughter Katelin and they agreed to meet at Deanne's place for dinner.

They arrived at Deanne's Place about the same time and Katelin said, "What is the reason we are meeting here? Is it something good or bad? Because, I got something good to tell both of you."

Kate always wanted to hear any story from Katelin, so she challenged her, "Tell us! We will tell you how our day went after we hear yours."

Katelin smiled gave her mom a trivial look and said," My group has performed better than any other group in the company both in sales and also in overall morale in the last opinion survey. Therefore, the President and CEO have promoted me to be the Senior Vice President responsible for sales all over the world," and she gave them her sweetest smile.

"I know you guys are going to tell me to make sure I don't overlook my health. I still have my monthly doctor's appointment so I'm obliged to go through the check-up whether I need it or not. This job also provides me with a free membership to a fitness center and I will be doing that twice a week, with of course, my 24-hour security and the limo and the driver, so I think at that rate I will be completely fine," she's giving them both a proud wink.

John and Kate were so proud and happy but John said with a stern look on his face and said," I can see you are thinking about our concerns before we even get to say them, which is nice, but you left out one important thing. The first thing your mother and I do every time we head an important project, we are finding the right people to fill in the positions in our team. If you have the right and good people reporting to you then your job becomes a lot easier."

"You will be getting calls from people you know asking you to hire them and you will need to review everything of each person. Get the background about their opinions on others, their jobs, how they get along with others, and their past performances. Make sure to get input from the President and CEO to see if you are in the same direction as them. If you take your time and make the right moves with people reporting to you then the job gets done much easier."

Kate looked at Katelin and sincerely said," You have seen what me and dad do at the beginning of our projects. So, you should listen to your dad but you also have to do what you think is right. You know that we are so proud of you and what you have accomplished, little or big," teary-eyed while holding Katelin's hand.

She added, "I must say I always knew you were the best, and that you could accomplish anything. It is fun for us to just sit back and watch you accomplish things. From the time you were little you would tell us what you wanted and then we would enjoy seeing you get what you wanted.

These things you told us you wanted to do were not small, but you made them happen.

John then described their upcoming trip, "We will be visiting different countries, meeting their leaders, for us." John was so serious giving all detail of their trip to Katelin.

John looked a little emotional because he always liked to see that mother-daughter relationship and conversation. He would like to see

Kate explain the details of the trip but Kate asked John to describe the trip. So John said," We will be away for two weeks starting this coming Thursday. We will be visiting different countries, meeting their leaders, and see how we can help them improve their ways in terms of security and other things in their countries, they would not do it unless we could show them why it should be done but now it has turned into a bigger thing. We will be meeting with Presidents, Prime Ministers, and Kings in several countries. We believe it has come down to them saying, we will do this for you, but you need to do something for us. " John was so serious giving all the details of what entails in the trip to their daughter. "You know we have stayed out of politics and that is why if some key people ask us to stand by them when they give a speech, we always make it a point that it's approved by many. People in our government want us to support them in their political campaign but we have politely declined in some ways. We will only meet and discuss with any country leader if the topic is safety for our leadership people and saving the entire mankind."

Katelin's eyes gleamed with tears and said," This can be a good thing. Send me your schedule and I can see if we can meet up someplace. Do you remember I said I was responsible for Worldwide Sales? Well, my position will be announced in several countries and I need to review their sales plans, which means I'm going to have to travel too!" she exclaimed in excitement Kate then said, "We cannot have our plans get into the press but maybe Natalie can work with your secretary and they can work something out and see if we can meet you halfway in a specific country."

The mother and daughter exchanged their secretaries' numbers. Katelin blurted, "Have Natalie call this number. I will let my secretary know that she needs to keep my trip private but try to work something out so we can be in the same country at the same time."

Kate had a tear in her eye and she said, "I guess what makes us feel so good is that you are so smart and beautiful you can do anything you want. Your dad and I can just enjoy watching you do so many things and be successful in what you do. Believe me when I say we have loved being with you since the day you were born," as she hugged her.

Katelin cried when she said," I know where I got this ability because I am so proud of both of you and I enjoyed watching both of you as well, do all these great things for the world."

John just enjoyed the mother-daughter scenario, it warms his heart, and feel like crying too as he said, "I love you both and I know I am lucky to have you in my life."

They then went home after a great and emotional night.

Meeting Katelin's Friends

John and Kate woke up early to do their morning exercise. Waiting for them at their bedroom was Katelin and she was upset. She was dressed in her running clothes. John and Kate have seen Katelin do this before. She would run with them because she needed to talk with them or needed them to buy something.

John looked at her and said," Ok should we run and you can tell us what you need or should we just go to the diner and we can discuss the problem."

Katelin just pointed to the door and said, "Diner!"

When they got to the diner Katelin told them about a man, she met who's doing some maintenance on their computers and he has worked for a firm that her company hired to make sure their computers stayed up and running.

So, John said, "That is a respectable job so what is wrong with fixing computers."

Katelin then said with a sad look on her face," He is a genius. He went out to dinner with me and my doctor friend and he knew more about medicine than the doctor did. When the doctor asked him how he knew all this, he just said he was reading a lot of medical books.

When he heard about the space project on TV that also interested him so he starting reading some electronics and calculus books and then tried to explain to me how it all worked. When I told him that most people don't pick up calculus, electronics and medical books and just start reading them. He just said he enjoys it. When I asked him if he ever thought about getting a job that can better make use of his skills, he just said he's happy where he is and he has friends working in the same company. Seems to me he loves his friends more than what he is capable of doing and that's just upsetting, you know." she almost cried as she expressed this.

"His friends told me they knew he is a genius and they hoped someday when they picked him up for work, he would be gone and off accomplishing great things. But he seems to be afraid to move on to a better job. I could not convince him to change his job and move up to make better use of his ability. I asked him if he would talk with you guys. He really likes and respects the work you are doing. I want you to convince him that he can do so much more."

Kate then said," I believe he should see a psychologist. But we will try to talk to him not because you asked us to do it but because we believe in you that he can be more."

"People have different timelines when it comes to working out their problems. Some just take days; others will take weeks to work it out. You do not know the story about us, do you?" Kate asked.

Then she narrated their story, "When they wanted us to work on a certain project, we would be at least 15 steps ahead of the project's impact. Almost every project we worked on; I knew it could have negative effects if used the wrong way. Your dad turned down more projects than he accepted because he can foresee the possible outcome if done the wrong way."

"If he's not ready to see a psychologist then we will meet with him tonight, at Deanne's Place, say at 7 o'clock? Remember he needs to make a decision, and whatever that decision be, it should be something that would make him happy."

They all ran back to the house and off their way to their respective jobs. The whole time Kate was talking to John saying," Do you think he has the same problems I had when my father was an alcoholic and would beat me almost every day?"

John just shook his head and said, " What is it with the ladies in this family? Can't you find someone that does not need help? I promise I will do my best to help this guy. You know Kate, you are better at handling this than me."

Kate was upset with what John said." It is important we give back if we can, right? We got plenty of help when we needed it. I saw an excellent psychologist that made me see it was not my fault for taking all those beatings when I was young. This may also help Katelin to see us as just two people that have flaws but were able to work our ways through them. Who would have thought that these memories would be brought back to our door steps?"

Kate with a faint smile, shook her head and said, "I was having so much fun just being the great Kate Colombo. I never thought I would have to think back to when I was called Kathy, but when I get to heaven, I guess that is what the Lord will call me if I am lucky enough to get to heaven," with sarcasm in her voice.

She realized it's a long day ahead of planning the trip, she went back to reality, "Ok, we need to get things finalized for this trip and try to anticipate where problems may occur. We also need to make sure all the US leaders are talking to the other leaders around the world and that they have a solution ready on any possible problems they can see."

When John and Kate arrived at the West Wing, they have to shift to work mode. They have to stop thinking about the young Johnny and Kathy that were dating and having fun at the beach with their friends from a long time ago as they have a big world that needed saving.

Then as they get to the conference room the first person, they see is the best man at their wedding is currently heading up the medical project, Paul Darma, who was also a psychiatrist.

They could not hold all the fun thoughts as they entered, and they both just laughed and John said, "Sorry Paul, we were brought back to our days when we were all young and just dating and then we saw you."

Paul just laughed with them and said," Those were the days my friends and I am glad you helped us get to where we are today. The numbers keep going up. We are saving many lives with this medical project. We did good!" Paul exclaimed with conviction.

John looked at Kate and both nodded YES to Paul, and then John with the exact timing asked Paul," How would you like to have dinner with us tonight?"

Paul gave John a surprising look and a wry smile," Why do I think we will be doing more than just eating food?"

John smiled back and said, "That is why you are the best, because you exactly know when we are going to have more than just a great dinner." John then went on to tell Paul the whole story about Katelin's friend.

Paul smiled and agreed "Ok, so let's do it. What time should I finish up? My guess it will be at Deanne's Place later?"

Kate with an appreciative look on her face said, "I think it will be at 7pm but need to have Natalie make sure everyone's calendar is free. She will call your secretary with the exact time.

Paul then said," I guess we are meeting now to discuss the upcoming trip? As I said we are ahead of all our projections on the medical project. The countries that we will be meeting with, will be very happy because of this project. Our country leaders in the Congress and Senate are also happy because the US is once again the inventor of things and are respected around the world. People around the world are looking at Capitalism as being the best way to bring about new things. The bad news is, we may have made some new enemies in other countries that do not agree on our way of governing."

John appreciated Paul's input," Thanks Paul, bring some charts on the trip that would show the numbers for each country. It would be good to also show comparatively the scorecard of each so they'd know how to do better. See you tonight. Katelin will bring her friend and we should have some fun and hopefully help someone," as he taps Paul's shoulder.

John and Kate were involved in meetings every hour throughout the day. The last meeting was with Jean who was setting up the trip. Natalie was also with her. Kate with a little smile on her face said,"

Jean it appears that we all have some pretty good stories to tell, sooner or later. We need them to follow one format and an overall scorecard that compare each country as to how they are performing. We can do a final review on the plane and if there are any changes required, we will be able to make those changes on the plane."

Then she also addressed her instructions to Natalie, "Natalie, you will be very busy on this trip too. If you think the other leaders' secretaries should be on this trip then let them know. What time is the meeting set up for tonight?"

Natalie responded quickly and said, "Everyone will be at Deanne's Place at 7pm so you better leave now."

They passed by Paul's office but he was already gone. The limo took them straight to Deanne's Place. It was exactly 7 o'clock when they arrived and Paul was already there but Katelin has not arrived yet. Just as they were getting out of their limo, Katelin's limo pulled over right behind them with her gentleman friend.

Katelin introduced them to Jeff Albright. As they were walking, Jeff looked at John and Kate with a smile and said," It is an honor to meet you both. I have been following all your projects from the beginning and I was so happy when Katelin told me you would be joining us." as he offered his hand for an honorable handshake.

As they reached their table Paul Darma stood up and gave Katelin a hug and extended his hand to Jeff and they shake hands." I have read about the Medical Project that you are heading up, Sir. The programming and managing of the databases are amazing. Also, all the agreements you have had to make all of it possible was outstanding," Jeff noted with so much delight.

Paul, with an astonished look on his face said, "What do you know about programming and databases."

Jeff responded by saying, "I like to do some programming in my spare time. I fix computers and most of the time it is not a hardware problem so I studied how to fix software issues until I became good at it."

Everyone then sat down and John started out the conversation by looking at Jeff and saying," Jeff which of the projects we are working on do you like the best."

Jeff responded quickly by saying," I like The Medical project the best.'

Jeff then went through every project and gave his reason why he liked the medical project. He confidently describes each project in detail.

They ordered their food and drinks and then Kate said with a very serious look," I understand you like the medical project among the rest. In fact, both John and Paul came up with it because they believed it would do good for most people who have any type of illness or condition. They knew how I suffered when I was young and it was around that time my abusive father and myself both realized where the problem was in my family. None of it was my fault. It took me a while to realize that all those beatings were because I did something wrong and it was my fault, but then when I found out it was not my fault, I gradually moved past it." Kate added, "These beating happened to both John and I. That is why when Katelin was born, John and I told each other to never give her a spanking." she looked and referred to Katelin. "If she did something wrong, I would give her a look without saying a word and her face would turn red because she knew she did something wrong and she would start crying.

Katelin is such a good daughter, that I rarely had to give her that look. She turned out perfect," with tears gleaming from her eyes as she said it.

Jeff began to have a tear in his eye and just said," How did you know I have an abusive father who drinks too much and when he gets drunk sometimes beats me? Most of the time he made me believe that beating me was to justify that it was my fault that something went wrong."

At that moment John got up and walked over to Jeff and told him "It is not your fault". John kept repeating that line over and over again until Jeff stood up and put his arms around John and began to cry and said," Is it alright to do this on our first meeting?" smiling in tears.

John responded jokingly," As long as you don't do this with my daughter."

Paul then stood up and walked towards Jeff, put his arms around him, and said,"

Would you come over to the Medical Project and work in the programming area? We could use your help and you would be helping a lot of people too."

Jeff with tears still in his eyes gave Paul a wide smile," Yes! it would be an honor to work on the medical project with you, Sir. I need to figure out what to tell my boss."

Paul responded, "What is your salary now."

Jeff told him his salary and Paul said," tell him I am doubling your salary and you will be working in the West Wing of the White House on one of the most important projects of the world. I think he will understand," as he tapped Jeff's shoulders.

Jeff then said quickly before anyone changed their mind, "I accept and will be joining your project in two weeks," with a mix of excitement and confidence in his eyes.

Katelin saw all of this happen tonight and she was in complete joy for Jeff and everyone. She turned to her mom and said," You never told me your story."

Kate just gives her daughter a smile that says, 'It's okay, I have forgotten everything already'. Katelin understood the message of her mother's smile.

There was a lot of discussion about the medical project while they were in the middle of their dinner and even continued right after. Paul suggested that Jeff read the book "Self Help and Mental Health a Tough Path to Wellness, by Nicholas Licausi" before he starts working on the medical project. It will help him a great deal and Paul has recommended that book to several people. Jeff has problems with insulin resistance and that book has many hints to reverse metabolic syndrome. This condition of insulin resistance has been known to be a contributing cause of schizophrenia, other mental illnesses and diabetes. Paul thought that book would help Jeff.

Katelin told her limo driver to take Jeff home and she would just take the ride home with her parents and Paul. Her security team along with John and Kate's security team follow them to their house in the Compound.

Katelin looked at her parents the whole way home and asked them more questions about their past. They both tried to explain to her and that it was not her grandparents' fault. It was a different time and a different situation. Those times if they did badly in school they would get the paddle. If they were bad at home, they would get spanked.

Katelin respected her parents more than ever. They have helped Jeff and so many others, just like how they help everyone working with them.

It was a happy night and a fulfilling one for the three of them.

The Help

Katellin was knocking at her parents' bedroom door with her running clothes on ready to start the day. The couple woke up and John opened the door and once again Katelin looked at them looking upset. John tried to greet her with a happy tone," Does this mean we are going to run to the diner and discuss something that's on your mind again?

Katelin smiled and said, "You know me pretty well. I need to talk to you about a couple of things before we all get to jet-set around the globe. I'll wait for you guys outside."

John and Kate got dressed right away and were always ecstatic when Katelin had something to discuss with them because they knew it is always an interesting problems and issues that John and Kate may have experienced when they were young.

Bill and the security team were waiting outside ready to run with them to the diner. There were four security guards and the Colombos family. As soon as they walked into the diner the guards posed at one table and the Colombos put some money in the jukebox and played some Willie Nelson songs while waiting for their breakfast.

Katelin then started in a serious tone," I am not sure what to do. I really like the doctor and now that I have gotten to know Jeff, I like him also. As you know with my new job, I will be doing a lot of traveling so I really do not have time to date right now."

John looked at Kate, almost saying but without saying it, this is your territory, I have no idea how to handle it. Kate looked at her daughter intently with a smile," One is very smart and really just starting out in life and the other is a doctor - pretty well established. Hmm...One thing you should know is that, whoever you choose from the two will be for love because I don't think all three of you needs money. So, pick the one that you love the most, the one that takes your breath away, and use your heart to make the decision. If you're not ready to choose right now, then enjoy being single and not in a relationship. Enjoy the solitude and dating at the same time and don't complicate your life with a relationship that you are not yet ready."

Katelin looked at her mother and said, "Wow! That's such a great advice, but I have another question. At work the current CEO and President has told me that in a couple of years she will be retiring and a couple of other people and myself are candidates for replacing her.

I like the Senior VP job I just got but would like to move up. What do you think I should do?" Katelin sounded like a child asking for a lollipop.

Kate looked at John and even though both could answer that question she thought John would do a better job talking to their daughter about it. So, John gave Katelin a serious look and said," Katelin most big companies have what they call an executive resource list. And I'm proud to hear that you are on that list. The way to move up is just to do what you have always loved to do. Perform well in your current position because people could fall off the list if they have a reason to. It was nice of the President and CEO to tell you that you were a candidate. She probably told other people on the list as well," he delivered it in the best reassuring voice he could have.

"The reason you got the Senior VP is because you were on that list with 3 or 4 other people and when the CEO's job opens up, they will pick the best person on that list and could also look at people outside the company. The reason you got your current job is because you were doing better than everyone else on the executive resource list."

"We are really happy to hear that you like your current job and are having fun. The people working for you and also your bosses can see that also, so keep up the good work and have fun at your job. You will do well at the company you are working for or if you decide to leave if you're not happy anymore, I am sure you will have plenty of offers from other Companies.

Katelin is loving the moment that both her parents are so into her and her welfare.

Then John continued, "Katelin, you are a very lucky person. You have two parents who love you dearly and would do anything for you. You also now have others that see you as your parents see you ever since you were born. You are a great person and will do a lot of good in this world and bring joy to a lot of people.

Just watch your health and don't miss to see the doctor every month just in case something pops up that needs to be taken care of immediately. One of the reasons your mom and I exercise every day is to keep our body healthy and that is also the reason why we have a regular monthly meeting with our doctors because when you get to our age there's always something new, they can find out about our health," as he carefully explained everything. But hey, this is another topic, that I won't discuss with you but I want you to discuss it with your mom and your doctor."

Then John moves a bit closer to Katelin and whispered, "Mom told me you were on pills so you would not get pregnant, that's okay, but you need to make sure you use protection from other diseases other people may give you. The pill does not protect you from other viruses. You need to use protection and you need to get the HPV shot."

Katelin then responded," I will always love you guys. You are the best parents anyone can have. Thank you so much for your help and advice." and she gave them a big hug.

Ready for the Big Trip

John and Kate got all their exercises accomplished on time and wanted to get to work at 9 o'clock so they could get all the final arrangements done. When they got to the West Wing, they stopped by Jim's office. He was in his office talking to Valerie.

When they got to the door to say Hi, he waved them into his office. Both Jim and Valerie had a big smile on their faces. John and Kate looked at each other and smiled because they knew they were in for a surprise. Jim then said, "Did you know that the President is getting a new plane? Well, I had a meeting with the President, and the heads of the Senate and Congress decided that we can't allow you to visit those countries on your list without having your leadership project plane. Either, we let you use the Air Force plane or have your own plane. So, it has been decided that your team should have your own. So, for this trip, you will have your new plane exclusive for your team, which is now being painted and upgraded to have some of the Space and Climate project gear installed.

We think you and your team will like it. The old Air Force One plane will now be called the Leadership Project Plane. Everything has been approved and it is yours."

John and Kate couldn't believe what they just heard and Kate muttered," Oh my God, thank you so much, Jim, we don't know what to say...it's...it's wonderful! On behalf of our team, we promise to take good care of this leadership project plane." They shook hands with Jim and excitedly left to go to their next meeting of the day.

Jean is leading the meeting since she was responsible for the overall trip. She facilitated the meeting in a very serious tone, "The leadership project plane is being prepared as we speak and has all the new pieces of equipment installed from the Space Project. I feel sorry for anyone that will try to take down this plane." then she proceeded with the schedules, "Your first stop will be London, and you will leave Monday morning.

You will stay there for 2 days and then proceed to Paris. While in Paris, many of the NATO Countries will be meeting with you. They have a proposal they want to discuss with you and we don't have any idea what it is at this time." She paused and made sure everyone followed, then continued, "Then you will fly to Moscow and then to Beijing. From there you will fly to South Korea where you will meet with both the North and South Korean President. Then off to Tokyo and your last stop will be Mexico City where there will be several Latin American leaders expecting to have a sit-down meeting with you."

"From there you will fly home to Washington D.C."

"You will spend about 2 days in each country. The main purpose will be to make sure they have the right security for all the leaders in their country. Bill will be auditing each of their security plans and a final meeting with each of their leaders, President, or Prime Minister to determine what needs to be done to pass the audit."

John signaled Jean that he would continue," Hey team, you might be wondering if all of the leaders in these countries agree with this agenda. Do some of them understand that we are visiting them because they are doing a good job and maybe we can learn from each other or are they expecting something from us?"

Jean nodded her head and answered in a firm tone, "They all understand that Bill and his team will be doing an audit on their security. We will also be doing a review on all projects and share best practices."

Bill stood up and started sharing the details," This trip is getting a lot of publicity so everyone will know where we are so we need to be extremely careful at all times. We will be bringing extra security with us on this trip. The President's older plane will be able to handle the extra security and also the press that will be coming with us. Many of us will be coming from the compound. We will have a convoy of limos and several security people to ensure that all the project leaders and the rest of the flying committee will get to the leadership plane before 10 a.m."

The meeting was adjourned and as they were heading out the door, they stopped by Jim's office to give him an update on the trip. They let him know the exact details of the trip just in case he needed to contact them. Jim said with a smile," I am confident everything will be fine on this trip because you have your own security and all the necessary modifications on the old Air Force One is now complete. I know you guys are making this trip to make sure proper security is in place for leaders all over the world. I also know when you both go on these types of trips many other problems get solved so the President and I are anxious to see what else gets achieved on this trip. You both always positively surprise us and you are making our country proud."

The meeting ended after 6 o'clock and everyone went home.

When John and Kate got home, they made love as soon as dinner was over and decided not to set any alarms for tomorrow. They plan to just relax and get as much sleep as possible because their next two weeks was going to be very busy.

A Family Weekend

John and Kate woke up at 9 am which was very late for them. John then said while they were both in bed," This is the latest we have ever slept. We must have needed the rest. Do you want the 2.5 hours of exercise or just run up to the diner in the gym and have breakfast?" he asked Kate dearly.

Kate replied still in her sleepy voice," I will check with Katelin and see what she wants to do."

Kate went to Katelin's room, opened the door, and noticed she was not in her room. She then went to the kitchen and noticed three cups of coffee and she saw Katelin brewing it for the three of them," Oh, good morning, how nice of you to be making coffee for us! You are the best daughter ever," and she kisses Katelin on the forehead.

Katelin handed her mom the coffee cup," Here you go, this one is for you. You can bring Dad's coffee with you inside. I know you guys are going to be away for a while so I skip work and just would like to spend quality time with my mom and dad."

Kate is amused by her sweetness," We are thinking the same thing. We know that two weeks is long before we get to do these things again in the morning, so we want to spend as much time this weekend with you as possible. Do you want to run to the diner with us and then maybe later go to watch a movie and have dinner at the Cheese Cake Factory?"

Katelin smiled and said," I would like to do all of that with you guys today. I will be ready in 30 minutes."

Kate went back into the bedroom with John's coffee and told him how sweet their daughter is," Our daughter made coffee for you and me. She knows we will be away for a while and would like to spend time with us, which is the same thought we have. She wanted to spend as much time as possible with us this weekend."

John is also touched with his daughter's sweetness and he's beginning to worry of being away from her," Okay we will run to the diner so we have time to talk and then go and watch a movie and then a great dinner after."

Kate then said," It was funny because Katelin and I were thinking the same thing when we woke up this morning. Go, get dressed, and we will leave in 30 minutes. I will let Bill and his team know ahead of our plans for today," as she heads out of the door.

John just smiled and in 30 minutes they were out the door and run their way to the diner. The Saturday for the Colombo family was very satisfying for the three of them. They had so much fun being together as family.

They ended up spending the entire weekend together. They knew that every time John and Kate went on a trip like this there is always an attempt on their lives. They all worried for each of them especially Katelin since she will not be with her parents.

Katelin wanted to talk to her parents as much as possible and spend every minute with them and on Monday she would be in tears just like a baby crying and she hugged them as tight as she could.

The Trips

Monday arrived, the day of their departure to visit other countries. John and Kate hurriedly completed their morning run and were on their way to the new leadership project Plane at 9 o'clock. The plane looked magnificent with its Leadership text printed on the side.

Somehow the information about the trip was leaked so there was a crowd of about 1000 people with banners and a lot of cheering on the ground. It was like the Beatles taking off and going on a trip. It was amazing because people in the government are usually not treated this way. John and Kate were like Hollywood stars.

As the Leaders are boarding along with several security people and several members of the press the crowd cheering goes louder. When John and Kate were about to board the plane, Jim arrived in his limo with lights and sirens along with two security cars. John and Kate walked over to Jim's limo and Kate said," Why all the lights and sirens, what's wrong?"

Jim in a very serious tone said, "The CIA received an intelligence that indicates an attempt on your lives before your first meeting in London."

John then said," Thanks for the heads up but no one can stop us. I have checked everything on this plane and I pity anything that tries to take us down. When we get to London, we will have the embassy security escorting us and all of us will be staying at the US Embassy in London.

Jim then responded and said," Well, we can't be too complacent.

Just in case, I have two F15 Air Force jets following you across the Atlantic," with his reassuring tone.

John and Kate boarded the plane and let everyone know what Jim said and encouraged anyone that does not feel safe to get off the plane. No one got off the plane because they knew if John and Kate felt safe then everyone would be safe.

It was nice to see the Leadership Plane with two F15s taking off and flying side by side with them to London. At about the aerial mid-point, everything looked calm and okay, the F15s turned around and went back to the US territory.

About 20 minutes from London two unidentified jets approached the Leadership plane and instructed it to follow them or they would be shot down. The pilot summoned John and Kate to the cockpit and told them about the situation.

Kate with a worried look on her face told the pilot to tell the jets to back off now or they would not be able to do it in a couple of minutes. The two jets got right behind the Leadership plane locked them as targets and were ready to fire their rockets. At that moment the pilot said over the radio," This is your last chance to leave."

Just as the jets are about to fire their rockets, the pilot disengages a device installed onboard from the Space project that is used in the Space Station destroying anything that is going to crash into the Space Station. When the jets were close enough to the Leadership plane, one was blown up while the other jet quickly turned around and left them alone.

As soon as the sky was clear with possible attacks, four British Jets showed up. Two told the Leadership Plane to follow them to an airport in London. The other two jets went after the plane that tried to shoot down the Leadership Plane. They shot down that plane. Then the four British Jets escorted the Leadership Plane to the London Airport.

Before the plane landed, John and Kate called Jim and let him know what happened and also told him that everyone on the plane was safe.

Jim said, "Since you have the press with you everything was

captured and can be televised and the whole world can witness the whole encounter. That device you have on the plane is amazing."

When the plane landed everyone on board cheered and applauded John, Kate, and the pilot.

When they got off the plane there was a huge crowd cheering with banners saying we love John, Kate, and the Leaders. They were like rockstars. No one from the Government has received this kind of welcome. Because of all the lives that are going to be saved by their projects the people around the world will love John, Kate, and the Project Leaders.

When everyone was on their way to the Embassy, Jim called John and Kate again and updated them, "We have traced the two jets and saw where they took off to intercept the Leadership plane. We bombed that airport since it looked like there were several other unmarked Jets there manned by Iranian soldiers. Please be careful because I do not believe that will be the only attempt in your life while you are on these trips."

Jim continued, "It is all over the news at the moment because of all the press with you on this trip, they know how to spread the news. I have Katelin here with me and she wants to know if both of you are okay."

Then Katelin's voice came on the line sounded so worried," Mom, Dad, thank God you are safe. Please be careful. You are the only parents I have," as she begins to sob.

Kate then said, "We love you honey. We will be careful. You be careful also, you are the only daughter we have. We will call you every night. Good bye for now," Kate almost cried as it breaks her heart to see Katelin upset and be away from her.

Jim then came back on the line and said," We have doubled the security on Katelin at the compound. Don't worry about her, she will be safe. Take care the two you are the best of the best that we have. I thought I would share that your daughter said she would never forget where she came from. She is also very proud of you saving the world. Bye for now and take care," then the phone got disconnected.

The US Ambassador in London picked up John, Kate, the rest of the Leaders and their security team escorted them to the Embassy. The press made arrangements at the hotel. The London Ambassador and his wife have John and Kate ride with them as they went to the Embassy.

The Ambassador told John and Kate," Everything was on the television. Everyone at the Embassy wanted to join us for dinner tonight. The Prime Minister will also be there."

As they approached the Embassy, they noticed that all of the staff were outside cheering as the Leadership team got out of the cars. Someone from the crowd chanted the USA hymn.

Everyone was proud of John and Kate most especially the Americans in London.

Everyone settled in first to their respective rooms. They have an hour to get ready for the formal dinner. The people working at the Embassy were advised that they can invite their families at the dinner party. Everyone wanted to see John and Kate.

Everyone got the surprise of their life. Not only did everyone see John and Kate but Prince William and his whole family came because his kids wanted to see them in person as part of their school assignment.

John and Kate made sure they had their picture taken with the Prince and his family so their kids could get a good mark on their assignment. They also gave the kids the art creation that Natalie's kids made. When the Prince's kids got it, they were so happy that they screamed for joy. The royal couple thanked John and Kate and their team, and their kids gave John and Kate a big hug and then roamed around enjoying the party.

At the dinner John and Kate noticed a large TV was set up so they knew they were in for a surprise. The Ambassador then got up and said," We have some guests who asked if they could join us at dinner."

Just then the TV was turned on and the White House dining room appeared with the President, Jim and heads of the Congress and the Senate via live satellite.

The President then got up offered a toast and said, "To John, Kate and the team for everything you did and will do for our country and for the world today. Again, you make us all proud to be an American. Also, the device that got rid of the jet that was trying to fire a missile at your plane. I want that installed on Air Force One. That was awesome. Once again, thank you and may you have a safe trip and let's all enjoy dinner!" and the President raised his glass, and everybody raise their glass too along with the shouting of 'Cheers!'

After dinner was over, John and Kate went to their room to get some rest.

They made love to cap off the night. Their first meeting is not until 1pm the next day and it is to review Bill's security audit for the security of the London Prime Minister and his staff. They set the alarm for 9 o'clock so they could get some exercise before their meeting and will still have plenty of time to be enjoying the sceneries of London from the Embassy.

They went to bed trying to forget that their lives were once again attempted to be taken from them.

The Security Review and The Surprise

John and Kate did their exercise within the Embassy compound. They were able to relax before their 1pm meeting, had brunch with the Ambassador and his wife. John looked directly at the Ambassador and asked, "What are England's greatest concerns? Also, we encourage you to attend all the meetings as much as possible because you and the Prime Minister can help us make sure that your leaders in England have good security and that your projects are also doing well."

The ambassador replied with a smile," Thank you John. I have cleared my calendar so I can assist both you and Kate while you are here. England's main concern is that they would like to have people like you and Kate and your entire leadership team that the country could look up to. If you think you have something that you could use England for as a partner, that would be great. England is used to being a leader among other countries. We have The Palace, the royalty family, the King and Queen. We have the Beatles for music. Now, at schools they teach about you and Kate as you can tell from the princes' children. They would like to be your partner in something that's greater than us, because it seems like you are partnering with many countries but have left out your best friend, England," as he said it in a very sincere tone.

Kate nodded in approval," We definitely want you in our meetings. We can see why the President picked you to be one of his ambassadors. We will see how these meetings go and we will take it from there, we may be able to come up with something helpful for your country."

Their lunch was about to end, and the meeting was due to start in about 20 minutes, so John and Kate went back to their room and made use of the few minutes left to freshen up. By 1 pm they joined the meeting and seated along with the US, British leaders and the Prime Minister, and as they walked in right behind them was the King of England. The King does not usually attend meetings but thought he also wanted to meet and work with John and Kate.

John and Kate did the things they are supposed to do when meeting a King. The Ambassador welcomed the King into the meeting and then reviewed the calendar with the King and everyone else.

The King said that he does not usually attend meetings like this but since the projects they will be discussing are of great importance to England and the World, he wouldn't want to miss it.

The Medical, Space, Storms, Earthquakes, Climate and Security projects are of great importance to England and its colonies.

"Our Prime Minister will take the lead in this meeting for England, but I want to hopefully add value to this meeting. I have one request, though, if I can invite the prince to attend this meeting as well?"

Everyone said YES out loud and in that instant the prince walked in and joined the meeting. The Ambassador nodded both John and Kate to stand up and John said," It is such a great honor to have so many important people in this meeting. Now, for a start we will give all of you the status of all the projects and also ensure we have good security for your leaders since they are so important to the country. I will add one more topic to this meeting and I am not sure of the answer to this question, but I hope by the end of this meeting we will have an answer. Let's come up with a project where US and England can partner together."

Everyone said YES out loud and was smiling. The Ambassador turned to Kate and whispered, "That is why you and John are such great people. You are a great influence on many."

Kate smiled and whispered back," Thank you. It was you who knows what everyone wanted."

John and Kate looked at the leaders' faces and could tell they were so happy they were part of something big in their country. Where else could they meet such important people? John in a louder voice," We are honored to have such important guests in our midst today. So, to review the security of your country's leaders let me present to you my colleague, Bill - head of our security, to give us the results of his security audit," as he pointed his arms towards Bill's direction.

Bill then stood up, a little nervous but security was a topic he knew better than anyone else in the room. With authoritative voice, he started his report," I will be telling everyone here things that terrorist would like to know so you must keep this information very confidential but also implement this within your network."

The Head of Security of England raised his hand and ask," What is your deepest fear?"

Bill answered," My deepest fear is, if something happened that will injure or kill a leader just because our security is weak and is easily breached. We need to stay one step ahead of terrorists or any other enemies. An example I can present was what happened to us on the way here when two unknown jets tried to destroy our plane.

We retaliated against their attack with something that was installed on the plane courtesy of our Space Program. A device that destroys anything that poses danger if detected by our space station. I would recommend England to have this installed on your leadership plane or royalty plane."

The Prime Minister waved his hand and said," I would highly agree to have that device be installed to some of our dignitary planes."

Kate looked at John and Bill and knew they would agree so she stood up and said," England is our most trusted partner. We can help you install that device and the other devices we have in the program, and you will just have to pay for the cost. Same with the Medical Project that we have, we will help you install on your computers and teach you how to use it, and the rest of our projects We will also help you use the earthquake and storm project items. Your project leader should be able to make that happen. England has been leading for many years and I believe it is something we all want to retain for your country; thus, we should build this partnership in that area."

Everyone was waiting for Kate to divulge her idea. Even John and the Ambassador looked puzzled. Then Kate said with a big smile," England controlled the sea years ago. They had the best war ships; fishing ships and the sea is something we need to fix. We can partner with England in coming up with a submarine that can explore the sea for food, minerals and anything else the world can use. We have a company that develops submarines, and we can have these experts create and customize a submarine that can best navigate the English seas."

The King then stood up and said, "I can see why your President and other country leaders trust you and John to lead these projects for the world. I will leave the decision to our Prime Minister, but you see we are so honored to have you as well. We are so happy that you picked England to be the first country to visit."

Everyone in the room is emotional with the King's message. The Prime Minister stood up and said, "I will gather my leaders and will appoint a leader to this sea project to work closely with as our official partner on this project. We have devices that can map the ocean and English sea territories. We also have programs in place that can give us the numbers and data of the number of fishes, turtles, plants and minerals and anything else under the sea. We have people in England that have been exploring everything that lives under the sea to ensure they can continue to live and multiply. I'm sure the people of England will be very happy when we announce this partnership."

The discussion moves to the status of each project, and everyone is relieved to know that the projects are right on schedule and are doing well.

After the meeting ended, the King invited the Prime Minister, The Ambassador, John and Kate for dinner at the Palace and even asked the Prime Minister and Ambassador to bring their wife. All of them accepted the invitation and they agreed to meet at the Palace in one hour.

The dinner was outstanding. They discussed every topic that was covered in the meeting earlier but went deeper into each topic. John and Kate are very honored to join the dinner with real people that have the power to change and make the world a better place. The dinner is focused on the discussion of how everyone can save the world.

It was getting late so John stood up and said," Thank you all for attending this meeting and I believe we have accomplished everything we wanted to accomplish. I look forward to getting the Sea Project started. I will brief our President, Congress and Senate to make sure we are getting the funds to build what we need. I hope that your project leader will also do the same thing. We will have another meeting about this in one week once we get back to the US."

John and Kate submitted the necessary paperwork requesting funds for and approval of the Sea Project. They also appointed a US Sea Project Leader that would be responsible for the project and get all the approvals necessary to move forward.

Before John and Kate got back to their accommodation in the US Embassy, the Ambassador set up another brunch for them before they went to the airport and took off to Paris. A dinner set up with the US Paris Ambassador is also waiting for them as soon as they arrive.

John and Kate went straight to their room, made love and decided not to set the alarm since the brunch is by 11:30 am.

So Long England, Hello Paris

John and Kate woke up at 8 am which was later than they usually do. They still did their full exercise. They showered, packed and got dressed for the trip to Paris. They went to meet the Ambassador dining room and it was packed with mostly the Ambassador's staff. John and Kate noticed a large screen TV, so they knew they were in for a surprise again.

The Ambassador stood up and cleared his voice," Yes, we have done it again. We have a little surprise for both of you and the rest of your team. The TV is then turned on the TV, and there on the big screen is the President, the leaders of the Congress and Senate all seated in a conference room.

The President then said, "Thank you for inviting us to your English brunch. We understand you had an important meeting yesterday with very important guests and you are going to seek our approval and funding to move forward with the Sea Project. We reviewed the paperwork you submitted, and you have our approval and funding to move forward with this very important Sea Project with England as our partner. We have talked with the Prime Minister, and he should have approval in England by the end of the day. The assigned project leader is sitting with us in this room and has been briefed to build her own team and immediately focus on getting it started. John and Kate, you are ahead of us again and that is why you are the US leaders and world leaders. You saw something that needed to be fixed and had already started working on it. When you saw it was ready to be taken to the next level with the right partner you asked for approval. You have been working with universities and private companies on your own and now you are ready to move forward. Thank you very much from the bottom of my heart and the entire American country. Keep up the good work and make your country proud!"

Everyone who joined the brunch and everyone in the conference room from the US including the President, stood up, cheered and applauded John and Kate. The couple stood up and gave their 'Thank You' speech. Once the applause subsided, everyone sat down and began to eat their brunch.

As John and Kate were shaking everyone's hands you could tell everyone wanted them to stay longer and that they are greatly honored of their visit. Their limos and security personnel that would take them to the Leadership plane are ready to take them and now everyone knows that the plane is one of the safest on Earth.

As the Leadership plane took off, both British and NATO planes escorted it to Paris. Even though they were probably not needed, it was to secure the Leadership plane from any attempt, so they sent 4 fighter jets surrounding the Leadership plane. The Leadership Plane landed first and then the NATO planes next. The British planes went back to England. It was a great sight to see and everyone on the Leadership plane including the pilot was honored to be aboard the Leadership plane.

When they got off the plane, several people are at the airport to meet them including the international press and media men and women. Another shining moment for John and Kate inspiring people around the world to respect people working for the government.

The US Embassy cars are ready and waiting to take them to the US Embassy in Paris. When they arrived at the Embassy all the staff were outside with the Ambassador and his wife giving them a warm welcome and all cheering as they entered the embassy.

The Ambassador came up to John and Kate and said and shaking their hands," Welcome to Paris! I can't wait to be sitting with you for dinner later to give you an update and brief you guys as to why NATO wanted to be a part of our Leadership meeting."

The Ambassador walked with John and Kate to his dining room. The other Leaders and the security are at the other dining area so they could sit with their counterpart leaders. Bill also started his security audit, so he would be ready to present the results first thing in tomorrow's meeting.

John was a bit upset when he said, "Mr Ambassador, we need to make sure our leaders in France are safe. The main purpose of the meeting was to ensure everyone will be safe and also get the status of all projects. What do you think the President of France and NATO would like us to do?" he sincerely asked the Ambassador.

The Ambassador looked serious and said," I believe he would agree with you and would do everything to ensure the safety of our Leaders. The results of your security audit will be very important. I understand he is going to present the results of the audit at 1pm tomorrow and right after that we can have our first meeting. I believe our NATO friends would like to discuss what you guys did in Asia, to bring peace to that region."

Kate then said, "Okay let's have the meeting at 1 pm. We will inform Bill his audit will be the first on the agenda and then we can have the Leaders give us the status of each project. We would leave the decision to you about the meeting with NATO. You can set it up and we will be there."

After their dinner, John and Kate were escorted to their room and they went to bed early to be ready for tomorrow's busy day. They also gave Katelin a call to let her know they were okay and she's fine as well.

The Security, Leaders and NATO Session

John and Kate woke up at 6 am so they could get in their exercise and brunch before meetings started. The Ambassador wanted to have brunch with John and Kate and the head of NATO at 11am before the meeting at 1pm.

They finished their exercise routine and were on their way to see the Ambassador. When they got to the Ambassador's private dining area, they noticed the head of NATO and also the President of France were there waiting for John and Kate to start brunch and the meeting.

When they walked in everyone stood up and the head of NATO spoke up and said," This is a topic everyone in NATO wanted me to discuss. We saw what was done in Asia and that really brought peace to that area. We also saw how you were brought peace between Russia and Ukraine. We do have reason to believe that something might trigger another war in Europe, and we don't want that to happen. Do you have any suggestions of what we should do?"

John stood up and said with a little smirk on his face," I believe it is time to see if you can get all the European and Middle Eastern nations to be a part of NATO. If you include Russia then they will understand the rules and will certainly not want to invade any other country," as he moves a step closer to the head of NATO. "When I say open NATO to any country, I really mean open it up. Allow countries like Egypt,

Israel, Iran and Russia, and others to have a chance to join. That way, countries like Russia will not feel like they are surrounded by NATO, or Israel will not be in constant fear of invasion or bombing. Because the idea of a country invading or bombing a NATO member country is like bombing all of the NATO member countries. It's like waging a war against the world, one country against many will surely lose. If you will allow Russia to join, then we will speak with them and see if they will accept.

The President who was very quiet in the room spoke up and said, "I like it and can see why both you and Kate are thought of so highly. You come up with great ideas."

Kate then said looking directly at the NATO Leader, "Get back to us today, if possible, because we are going to Russia tomorrow, and that's something we can include in our agenda when we talk to their leaders. I believe we can talk it out with them, the idea of joining NATO.

While the discussions were ongoing, everyone was eating their brunch in the middle of it all. It's almost 1 pm, the Ambassador stood up and said, "Our 1pm meeting is due to start in about 10 minutes. Everyone is invited to proceed to the meeting hall where we will be discussing security and the status of the Medical, Storm, Sea, Climate and Earthquake projects."

Everyone attended the 1 pm meeting except the NATO Leader since he had to get an answer from the NATO team for John and Kate. As they were walking to the conference room the President of France said," I hope you don't mind me attending the next meeting but since all your projects affect France, I want to make sure our country is doing all we can to make these projects successful.

Both John and Kate smiled and appreciated his attendance. When they got to the meeting, everyone greeted John and Kate and then they all sat down. John remained standing and said," First of all, I would like to acknowledge the presence of the President of France in this meeting. All the projects are important to France, and I want to start the meeting by asking each of the project leaders from the US and France to please stand up and give us the status of each of the project, starting with the medical project leaders," then he sat down.

The two leaders stood up and the French leader gave the complete status of what is happening in France and the impact of the medical project. He highlighted in the report, "Everything is going well, and the number of deaths has been reduced from last year. All precautionary measures were very positive." everyone applauded, and the French project leader took her seat. Then the US Leader gave a world view of the measurements and deaths on a global scale.

All project leaders did the same thing until each project was all reported. It was getting late, Bill delivered his Security audit status and report, the last. France passed the audit except for a few things they acknowledged that needed to act and address immediately.

The meeting ended at 7 pm. The NATO Leader showed up towards the end of the meeting. Kate asked," Do you have an update from your NATO Leaders concerning their approval of our recommended changes?"

The NATO Leader replied, "They liked your recommendations so would you talk to Russia about joining NATO and let them know we will be expanding NATO and allowing other countries to be a member of. "

Kate gave her reassuring answer," We will talk to the Russian leader tomorrow. As soon as Russia gives us an answer, then you need to start talking to other countries as well. We will give you a call tomorrow and then we can plan things out on how to convince the other countries to join NATO."

John and Kate had a very hectic day. Right after everything, the meeting, the dinner, finally they were back to their accommodation room.

As soon as they got back to their room, they called Jim to give him an update so he could also update the President.

They need to wake up early tomorrow to get in their exercise before their flight to Moscow, Russia at 11 am.

They made one last call before they'd call it a day. They called the US Ambassador in Moscow and updated him of their arrival and asked him to set up a meeting by 5 pm on Friday with Andre to discuss the NATO proposal.

All is set for France, and they have accomplished what they all came for. One mission after another. With that in mind, John and Kate slept peacefully that night.

The Meeting with the Russian Leaders

John and Kate woke up before 6 am so they could get in their exercise and have breakfast with the Ambassador and the other leaders by 9 am and then be at the airport for takeoff at 11am.

When John and Kate walked in for breakfast, they were surprised to see all the Leaders, the President of France, the NATO Leader and some press joining. There was no large screen TV, so they knew there were no big surprises. When everyone was seated, the President of France stood up and said," Thank you for coming. It is always a pleasure to meet people like you and the rest of your team. My family and the rest of the country have benefited from some of your projects, and we are grateful for that. I spoke with your President last night and we are both in agreement with the direction NATO is taking. I hope we can make it happen." A big applause was heard in the hallway.

Kate looked at John and then stood up and responded to the President, "Thank you for being a part of this meeting, Mr. President. John and I were very happy with the progress of all the projects here in France. There were a few recommendations made by our security team which I am sure your team will implement. We will do our best to implement what we discussed yesterday concerning NATO. I want to thank the Ambassador for hosting this event. Au revoir, everyone!"

Everyone got up, shook hands with Kate and John and they sent them off in a round of applause.

Then the team proceeded to the airport and the Leadership plane took off for Moscow, Russia.

The Leadership Plane was such a site to see as two NATO fighter jets escorted them to Moscow. When they reach the Russian border, four Russian Jets took over and escorted them to until they landed in Moscow.

That transition was a beautiful sight to see. Since the press was on board the Leadership plane it was all captured and shared with the World. A message that signifies that the Leadership plane is formidable and there's no stopping them.

When the plane landed there was a Russian crowd of close to a thousand people gathered to greet and welcome them as they all got off the plane. Their cars are waiting complete with Russian security personnel to take them to the American Embassy in the center of Moscow.

They left the private airport secured by Russian security and it was such a beauty to witness Russians protecting Americans to make sure no harm will come to them.

When they got to the US Embassy, the Ambassador and his wife greeted them in their Russian way of welcoming guests along with their Embassy staff. As John and Kate got out of their limo there was a loud cheer from the people around. John and Kate were overwhelmed by the warm welcome, so they just nodded their heads and thanked all of them.

The Ambassador updated them that Andre is coming to the Embassy for the 5pm meeting as planned and may join them for dinner. Since the meeting with Andre was in about an hour, they were shown to their room to settle down. They called Jim first to inform him of their safe arrival in Moscow and updated him of the plans and agenda. Then, they called Katelin back home to check with her and told her as well that they were safe and fine.

Jim told them they saw the jet escorts from Paris to Moscow. The President called the Russian President and thanked him for doing it. Jim updated them that the President had no news to give them as of the moment and he just wishes for all of them to be safe.

When Katelin was on the phone, she jokingly said," I told you guys, that you are going to be famous one day. Your trip has been closely televised by the media, so you don't have to tell me everything that's happening on your trip. I just want to make sure both of you are getting enough sleep, eating well and safe so you can come back home intact."

She was on a speaker phone, and they could hear her laughing and then John said," I knew this day would happen. Our child is now our parent and we're hearing the words from you, that's just so sweet. We missed you so much honey."

Then Katelin laughed and said," Okay, then. Good luck with your meeting and make sure our leaders in Russia keep you all safe and the NATO agenda would turn out well. You are truly changing the world. Love you guys."

John and Kate thanked Katelin and Kate said," You can always make us laugh and make us feel good, and we need that right now since we are away from you. We got to go honey for our first meeting. We love you too. We'll call you again soon."

They went to the conference room for their meeting with Andre and the Ambassador and as soon as they walked in, Andre and the Ambassador stood up and offered them handshakes. They then all sat down.

John brought up the topic of the original purpose of the meeting which was to do a security audit and to also get a status report on all the projects all scheduled for tomorrow at 1 pm. Bill has enough time for his security audit.

John wanted to also clarify the purpose of the meeting, so he asked," Andre I need to bring up the NATO topic. We were not planning to discuss this topic right now, but since we believe having Russia be a part of NATO is important, so we might as well get involved." He opened it up then. "This way, any country can support each other including Russia in the event of attack or invasion. Trading between Countries would also be improved. We thought this would be good for Russia and also peace in Europe and other countries."

Andre smiled and said," I agree with you John. I will talk to our President and see if he agrees of the idea. Has NATO agreed to let Russia join? What other Countries will join NATO?" Andre was curious to know.

Kate responded to Andre's question," All European and the Middle Eastern countries. This includes Israel and Iran which NATO will also invite. Any country that would attempt to attack any NATO member would be in trouble with NATO. Any Country that would drop a bomb on Russia or try to invade Russia then they would be in trouble with all the member countries of NATO including USA."

Andre nodded," I will get back to you by tomorrow with an answer from the President of Russia." as he gave them a reassuring look.

The Ambassador then said, "It is already 7pm. Andre would you like to join with us for dinner?"

Andre said," I would like to, but I have a lot of work to do so I will see you all tomorrow for the 1 pm meeting. I will answer by then," and he exited from the meeting hall.

The Ambassador then said," Call us at any time if you need to clarify anything. I look forward to seeing you tomorrow at 1pm."

Everyone stood up and said good-bye to Andre and was also asked if he could join them for brunch at 11:30 am the next day. He said he would and hoped to have an answer by that time.

Then dinner was brought in. The Ambassador planned the dinner well for John and Kate.

After dinner they went to their accommodation room and set their alarm for 6 am so they could get some exercise before the 11:30 am brunch.

The Meetings that Could Change the World

John and Kate woke up to the sound of the alarm, 6 am. They get into their usual morning exercise. They prepared themselves for the brunch with the Ambassador.

They went to the Ambassador's private dining room and the Ambassador was there already when they walked in, and the Ambassador greeted them good morning." Let's hope that Andre was able to talk with the President and convince him in joining NATO. He called me and said he will be late in a bit since his meeting with the President was at 10:30am," the Ambassador said.

John and Kate sat down, and the butler brought them coffee. Kate raised her cup and said," Let's toast to Andre and hopefully, he was able to successfully convince the President in making Russia a part of NATO." Just then they noticed that the butler was leading someone into the dining area. Then they all looked at the entrance to the dining area and there was Andre and standing beside him was the President of Russia. Andre with a smile then said," I hope you don't mind; I brought a friend of mine to our brunch."

Everyone stood up and the Ambassador said in a surprising tone," What an honor, Mr. President! Welcome to the Embassy! I believe you know John and Kate Columbo."

John and Kate then rushed up to the President and shook his hand.

John then said," Thank you so much for sending the jets to escort us here in Moscow."

The President then said with a smile," Oh, don't mention it. It was necessary for your safety. And I hope you don't mind but I am going to have the same jets to escort you to the China border. I thought I would come to this meeting myself because I always enjoy meeting the both of you. I understand you both believe it is a good idea for Russia to join NATO. Andre also thinks it is a good idea. If it was anyone else, I would not even consider it because I trust you three and you truly recommend things because you believe it will help Russia. I also believe it is a good idea. We will join NATO," as he looked into the faces of John, Kate and the Ambassador.

The people of Russia will be happy with this decision. They were starting to feel isolated because of the Ukraine problem. We do not need any more land.

"With your Climate project we have more land that we can use, and we do not need anymore. Also, if any country would try to take our land it is nice to know other countries will come to our aid. Believe me, when I say it felt good to make sure you landed in Moscow safely. Now, Russians would be prouder to be Russian again, and when I got a call from your President, he thanked me, which means Americans liked Russians which is fantastic. From now on, when you come to Russia you must see both Andre and me. I will clear my calendar for you. The people here in Russia believed in both of you just like Rock Stars. Your projects have saved many Russian lives," and he remained smiling as he was saying all of this positive feedback.

John and Kate felt happy and proud upon hearing all the things the Russian President said. "Thank you for the kind words and wonderful compliments, Mr. President. We believe you are making the right decision in joining NATO. Your presence will make it to be one of the most powerful organizations in the world and no other country will try to attack any NATO country members."

The Ambassador then said with a big smile," At this great moment,

I would like to make a toast with everyone at this table. We need something stronger to make this type of toast," he laughed as he raised his coffee cup to initiate the toast. Just then, the butler opened a bottle of Vodka and poured it for everyone.

Then the Ambassador raised his cup again this time with the vodka and said, "This is to Russia joining NATO and also the health of everyone in this room." They all drank until the glass was empty.

Then they all sat down and ate their brunch. It was almost 1 pm and the next meeting was about to start. Andre attended the meeting along with the Russian and American project Leaders. The Russian project leaders were right on schedule in all of the projects. The security was as good as the US and even had some ideas that the US could make use of.

It looked like Russia was doing well on all projects and Andre, John and Kate were all pleased with everything that's presented in the meeting.

The meeting ended at 7 pm so everyone had a late dinner together and then they all called it a night.

John and Kate went to their room, gave Jim a call for updates on everything that had been discussed in the meeting. He was very pleased. They also called the NATO Leader to let him know he could now start recruiting other countries and include Russia as a member in NATO. He was also very pleased. Everything went as planned.

They made their last call for Katelin. She was currently in a board meeting so they called her cellphone because if they called her work number they would have to go through a few people. Kate said, "It is mom and dad, and we have you on speaker."

Katelin said, "Hey, I was in a meeting earlier when you guys called. But when I got your message, we all agreed to take a break for a few minutes. Everyone cheered when they all knew it was you guys calling me from Russia. They all knew you guys. You are on TV almost every night. The Russian jets escorting you to Moscow was the latest and now I am hearing on some networks are reporting that Russia is becoming a part of NATO. Do you guys ever rest? You should ask for a raise," feeling so proud of her parents.

John and Kate laughed and said," You always make us laugh. How come they have you working Saturday?"

Katelin laughed and said," The same reason you are working on Saturday. There is work that needs to get done. It is a great job, and I am having fun. Our team is making a difference in this company. The stock is going up which means we are all a lot richer. Tomorrow is Sunday and I will be going to church and maybe watch a movie with my doctor friend."

Kate then said, "We are both very proud of you. We will be in China tomorrow. You better get back to your meeting. It was great talking with you. Be safe and take care, we love you always!"

Katelin reassured her parents," I am always safe because, apart from my company's security, a limo with my own driver, now Jim has assigned some more security also, so, I will be okay. I love you both. You both take care and be safe too."

John and Kate will have about an 8-hour flight tomorrow from Moscow to Beijing. They could sleep late since the plane departs at 1 pm. They did not set any alarms so they can sleep as much as they want to. The Ambassador wanted to have Brunch at 11am so they had enough time.

John and Kate made love and went to bed.

From Moscow to Beijing

John and Kate woke up at 7 am so they could do their exercise will have brunch with the Ambassador and Andre before the Leadership plane was scheduled to leave. The Ambassador was there with his wife, so John and Kate joined them, and Kate said," On my next visit here, I want to do some shopping."

The Ambassador's wife responded and said," Of course, you should. We'll do it then.

I know a few spots I think you will like."

Kate smiled and said, "Okay it's a date then."

This was the first relaxing brunch they had had in a long time. Just small talk and great food. Then Kate said," I hate to stop this conversation, but I think it's time to leave," she whispered to John.

Kate stood up from the table and said, "Thank you so much for hosting this for us. It is the most relaxed brunch John and I have been in. The Russian leadership team is in good shape as well as your security except for a few things that needed to be fixed."

A convoy of VIP cars with Russian and US security were waiting to take everyone to the airport. When they got to the airport the US and Russian press were there plus around 1000 people cheering for John and Kate and the leadership team as they say their 'bon voyage' wishes. Everyone got onto the Leadership plane, and it took off along with two Russian jets escorting them on both sides.

When they reached the China border, two Chinese jets were in position to escort them, and the Russian Jets returned back to Russia. It really looked fantastic. The press on the plane got the whole thing on film. It is probably the only time where you have seen the US, Chinese and Russian aircrafts all in the same picture and the Chinese and Russian jets were both there to protect the US Leadership plane.

The Leadership Plane and the two Chinese Jets landed at the same time and parked next to each other at the airfield. The US Ambassador to China meet them at the airport to pick them up.

When they arrived at the embassy, there was a large crowd greeting them. Everyone was cheering and yelling John and Kate's names. They have a handful of fans in China as well.

On the way to the Embassy the Ambassador told John and Kate their first meeting will be Monday at 10 am. The Security people will be doing their audit tonight and in the morning. They will present the audit results at around noon.

When they were almost at the Embassy the Ambassador got a call from his secretary and he thought he should take it. The call was connected to the President of China and the President invited the three of them to the Palace for dinner. Kate and John heard the conversation so both motioned for the Ambassador to accept the invitation. The Ambassador told the secretary that they had just arrived from the airport but would be happy and honored to join him for dinner at the Palace.

They quickly called Jim, the US Presidents most reliable person and their friend. Jim had no idea except China is getting some bad press about the way they are building their Army and some rumors that they are stealing in the Security and IT area.

As they drove up to the Palace the Secretary General was at the door to meet them. They had an excellent friendship with the Secretary General. They all greeted each other, and the Secretary General took them to the President's dining area. They all greeted each other and then the President asked John and Kate in a very serious tone," I trust all of you to tell me the truth on a question that has been on my mind. The US papers printed that China is stealing all of the U.S. secrets.

All Countries steal things from each other one way or another. Your CIA agency steals information. We both do the same thing but China is made out to be the bad country. They also say we are taking over all the manufacturing jobs and we are putting American people out of work. Your US Companies came to us to do manufacturing so they can sell goods to the US people at a cheaper price. In your country, this is called capitalism. There was a company in the US called Digital Equipment Corporation (DEC). They were put out of business because their competitors manufactured products cheaper and solve problems for their customers faster. "

The President continued, "The question is how do we get your press to stop printing things about China that makes us look bad? Some of the things are not true and even if it is, it's a reality that most countries do for economy's sake. You and Kate seem to have solved a lot of world problems. How do you do it?" as he looked at John and is waiting for an honest answer.

John and Kate looked at each other, and Kate nodded at John to give the President an answer that he's looking for.

Republic of China is one of the respected countries in Asia. John addressed the President's question in a very sincere manner, and said," We pick very carefully the projects that we need to work on along with the right partners to work with and the best people to work with us. These projects are formulated and created based on world issues and we make sure these projects would give a positive impact to the world. They are Projects that will help the people and the government. These things are for the world to at least make it a better place when these projects are completed. We believed you had very positive news today because you protected and escorted our landing to your territory. You got very positive press when you also signed the Asia Trade Agreement (ATA)." John doesn't know if his answer is satisfying to the President.

"Your leadership team has people on all of our projects, and you are leading among other countries based on our scorecard which we will present and share to you, Mr. President in time. These are projects that puts China at the top and in helping the world. "

"It takes time, but you are headed in the right direction. People around the world are seeing China as a country that is not trying to conquer the world, but a Country that is trying to make the world a better place and is a very strong country. I believe if you can find a project that would help the whole world then that would help China's image. We will also show how your work on the Leadership Projects has helped the World."

The President of China then looked and John, Kate and the US Ambassador and said with a smile," That's very insightful, John. I won't be attending your meeting, but my Secretary General will attend on my behalf. Whenever you come to China, I want you to visit the Palace if you got time, it's open for the both of you. Now, let's have dinner and some entertainment." Several people joined them and there was a great deal of food. All vegetables for Kate since they were informed, she only ate vegetables.

When dinner was over, John and Kate finally got to the Embassy accommodation a little after 10 pm so they called Jim for an update, and then called Katelin to let her know they arrived just fine in China.

Then they went straight to bed and set the alarm for 7am so they could get in a little exercise before their first meeting at 10 am tomorrow. They have accomplished the things that are needed for today.

China Projects Review

The couple woke up at 7am for their morning exercise and a short breakfast. Their first meeting is at 10 am. They ran around the Embassy grounds and on their way back to their room they passed by at the conference room for their 10am meeting, and noticed some coffee, juice and danish so they quickly popped in the room and grabbed some juice and headed back to their room to shower and get ready for the meeting.

They were ready by 9:30 and knew where they could get some coffee and snacks, so they went straight to the conference room. It seems like most of the Leadership team are doing the same thing. John and Kate did not start the meeting but figured they would let everyone talk amongst themselves since many of the US and China project leaders have not gotten to know each other personally. They only exchanged emails or seen each other on zoom calls but this is the first time they have met face to face. It's nice to see Chinese and Americans interact with one another.

John and Kate always liked to meet people over a meal and usually they were able to really find out about people this way, and if they had a problem, they would let them know. They enjoyed the getting-to-know discussion until 10 am when the meeting was about to start. The Ambassador and the Secretary General of China just walked into the room, grabbed some coffee and sat down, ready for the meeting.

John then stood up and said, "I am going to ask Bill the Security

Leader who is doing a security audit to give us the results of the audit here in China. After which, the Project leaders will provide updates and status for each project." John sat down and allowed Bill to take over.

Bill got up and said," Thank you John and Kate. Well, China has put all their leaders and also their security in a Compound similar to the US. We are now checking to make sure proper security is also followed for document protection. There are rules that must be followed to protect all information on Computers and any types of data or information. We have provided the security team of China the basic education in this area which I believe, they will implement."

Right after Bill's report, each project leader gave and completed their project status report and updates on their designated projects.

John and Kate then took over and discussed other important matters in the meeting after they got a complete update on each of the projects.

Towards the end of the meeting, the Secretary General of China expressed that he's very happy with the status of all the project, and that he believed that these projects would be a big help to China and the World.

After the meeting was adjourned, John, Kate and the rest of the U.S. team went to their rooms since it was already 8 pm, and their flight to South Korea would be at 11 am. After they all had their dinner, they each settled in their room to rest and sleep.

In most travel days John and Kate always set their alarms in the morning. They set their alarm at 7 am so they could get some exercise, before traveling to Seoul, South Korea which is a 2-hour flight.

Since it was a bit late, they just dropped Jim an email with the status and updates in China. They also asked their secretary in the US to set up the meetings in Seoul. Of course, they can't forget their daughter, Katelin. They just sent her a message saying they were doing fine and that they can't make a call as it is a bit late in China and they needed to rest for another flight the next day.

They went to bed feeling a bit exhausted with all the jet lag they had acquired and the fast-paced meetings they had had for the past week. They sleep with the thought that they will soon be home.

The North and South Korea Projects

John and Kate woke up at 7 am, did their exercise and proceeded for a quick breakfast meeting with the Ambassador. They were wrapping up their discussion about their visit and the Ambassador looked forward to their next visit.

At 11 am, everyone got into their limos and a convoy of cars headed to the airport to board the Leadership Plane. There were 5000 people at the airport that were cheering for John, Kate and all the Leaders. When the plane took off to Seoul, South Korea, there were 2 Chinese Jets that took off with them.

It was really a beautiful sight to see the Leadership plane and the 2 Chinese Jets taking off together the South Korean jets take over in escorting the plane as they entered the Korean air space until they landed in Seoul. Another crowd greeted them at the airport, but they were kept at a distance. In every country that they have visited, there have been large crowds that cheered for John and Kate and the leadership team.

The US Ambassador to South Korea met John and Kate as they got off the Leadership plane and directed them to their exclusive cars along with the rest of the team in a convoy. On their way to the embassy, the Ambassador told them that the 2 Korean Presidents asked the three of them to join them for dinner at the Blue House by 7 pm. The President of South Korea lives and works at The Blue House.

Since it was only 2 pm they decided to go to their accommodation at the US Embassy to rest, settle down and prepare for their series of meetings in Korea. After a couple of hours resting, they then prepare themselves for the meeting with the 2 Korean Presidents. When ready, they got into the embassy service car and headed to the Blue House.

When John, Kate and the Ambassador arrived at the Blue House, the North and South Korean Presidents went out to greet them and the South Korean President greeted them with a smile," Welcome to the Blue House. We are so happy to see you again. While we were waiting for you, we were discussing possible projects we could work on together as partners. I hope both of you will give it some thought. Let's go in and have something to eat and drink and then we can discuss," as the President ushered them in.

As they sat down, entree drinks and appetizers were brought in, John said with a smile," Kate and I were thinking about building a device we can use for the Sea project. Would both of you like to partner with US and England? The US government planned to build a submarine that would be able to go under the North Pole and can explore on ice. Since you both are good at building cars, you would probably be the best to build the next generation submarine that could travel to the bottom of the sea. We could use it to look at all the possible aquatic problems in the Pacific and provide resolutions on it. Right now, we have England getting ready to mine the areas in the Atlantic and other areas close to it."

"We just started the Sea Project. We want to mine and explore using the submarine. A trip to the bottom of the sea and doing a great deal of mining is something that has not been focused on before. So, this submarine will have to be built for that purpose. If both of your countries are interested, then we will have you on board and put you in touch with the US Sea Project leader along with the England Sea Project leader."

The North and South Korean Presidents discussed it for a while and then the North Korean President said," Alright, it is a purposeful project, count us in. We will work with other Sea project leaders. Thank you for presenting this opportunity and having us be a part of it."

John quickly responded," I believe it would be great if you could mine under the polar ice pack. We use a lot of rare metals in our phones, cars and other things. It's money you can make by selling some of these rare metals and use it to invest into the Sea project."

When the dinner and discussion was over John and Kate said, "We will review all projects tomorrow at 11am and also the security audit that is being conducted earlier for the leaders in each of your country."

The South Korean President said, "We would not be able to attend but will be sending our representatives. The next time we discuss this type of topics and review we will be in North Korea."

The couple smiled at the thought of being in the North Korea. John then said with a boyish grin," We always enjoy talking to both of you. We are not sure when the next one will be, but we will definitely plan this again. We did this one because we thought we needed it. We will say goodbye for now and hope to see both of you soon. Always remember you have our personal phone numbers so call us if you need something taken care of."

John and Kate waved goodbye to the Korean presidents.

John, Kate and the Ambassador got into their service car and the Korean presidents send off several police and security cars escorting them back to the US Embassy. On their way to the Embassy, they called Jim and gave him a complete update, including the review tomorrow and reminded him as well that they would be leaving for Tokyo the day after once the reviews and audit are complete.

When they got to their room at the Embassy it was about midnight, so they called Katelin because they were thinking she would be on her lunch break. When Katelin answered her cell phone, her voice was excited as she said," Hey both of you, I am tracking you as you are going around the world. It's almost the same trip we took when we lived in Tokyo and went around the world except that we did not have our own private plane and jets escorting us from various countries making sure we stay safe."

"The press have captured really well the part where China jets being relieved by Korean jets. Also, we did not get to stay in an Embassy accommodation, so your trip seems a lot better except that, both of you are working, and we were on vacation then."

Katelin was on the speaker phone so she could hear them laughing in the background, then Kate stopped laughing for a minute and said," It is always fun talking with you, honey. You always make our day."

John butted in, "You are not a good joke teller, but your stories always make us laugh. I guess we do have great memories. We just called to tell you we are fine, but I guess you know that from the news. Also, we wanted to make sure you are okay too. How is your new job and did you meet any interesting people?"

Katelin answered," The new job is great. I need to get used to having security around all the time, and a limo with the driver. They are being extra careful because they did have a board member kidnapped a year ago. I have gone out with the Doctor friend a couple of times. He is a lot of fun. I really enjoy everyone I work with. We go out to lunch every day. In fact, they are waiting at my door right now, so I better cut this short and say thank you for checking up on your only daughter and making sure she is okay. You guys, be careful and have a good night's rest. You deserve it. Love u both, always."

Katelin could hear her dad in the background wishing her well to have a great lunch. They both hung up.

John and Kate called it a day, complete and fulfilling. They set their alarm back to the usual - 6 am.

A Day in Seoul, Korea

John and Kate woke up at 6am to start their day with an exercise and also had time for a quick breakfast in the Embassy cafeteria with the Ambassador, and then started their reviews at 11am. They were able to get their run on the Embassy grounds and then they went back to their room, showered and dressed for their meeting.

A butler was waiting for them when they opened the door and said he would show them to the area where the Ambassador was waiting for them to have breakfast together. The Ambassador is with his wife, greeted John and Kate with a pleasant morning.

When Kate was introduced to the Ambassador's wife, she gave her a big hug and said," If these guys are done with whatever they are doing today, I want to take them to do some shopping," as she was excited to take Kate to the heart of Seoul.

"Do they still have night shopping in Seoul?" Kate asked.

The Ambassadors wife said, "Yes they do. Why don't you let me set something up? We can have dinner, and then do some night shopping and spend a warm evening wandering around the Seoul night market, with Myeongdong Night Market and Dongdaemun Night Market being the front-runners. They both have decades of history and multiple layers to them."

John and the Ambassador looked and each other and nodded their heads so Ambassador spoke up and said," Is it OK if John and I join you ladies for your night shopping tonight?"

The Ambassador's wife and Kate looked at each other too, and they all agreed to have a wonderful night later so the Ambassador's wife said," Sure it will be a double date and fun then." And the couples started to enjoy their breakfast full of excitement.

Kate knew from living in Tokyo and being an American can be very lonely and the only fun was when other American wives would get together and do something. So, Kate had a big smile on her face, and she said," Yes this will be fun. We need to be careful because I remember John getting into a discussion one time and they led him to a dark alley because the watch he bought was not working and they wanted to fix it. Well, they did fix it, but I thought I had lost him for a minute," she smiled as she shared that story.

The Ambassador then said with a serious voice," Don't worry we will have plenty of security. I'm sure your other leaders and your security team would want to join us when they find out about this. Let's try to keep this shopping to ourselves until we actually leave so the bad guys wouldn't have the time to prepare to do harm," and they all laughed.

Everyone agreed, and it was almost 11am so John, Kate and the Ambassador headed to the conference room. The 2 representatives sent by the President from North and South Korea, plus the Korean project leaders and the US project leaders were already seated. John noticed Bill, who was ready to present his security audit results, smiling at him.

John started the meeting in a very serious tone," Good morning, everyone and thank you for coming. The first order of business in today's meeting is to hear the results of your security audit, to be presented by Bill, which is followed by updates on the status of each of the projects. Bill are you ready to give us the results of your Audit for North and South Korea?", Bill nodded, and John took his seat.

Bill had some charts prepared so he got up and showed everyone the results. The results showed that they were both following the US model of security and have built compounds but they both needed to work in the right way to protect the information that they have on their server.

Then each of the project leaders got up and gave a status on all projects. All the projects were on schedule.

There were 2 items that John asked about and which were of concern. It appears that the reduction of deaths using the Medical Project Computer was not as great as in the other countries. The Korean Leaders thought this was due to the fact that Koreans do not eat the same food as other countries. John said he will look at Japan and see if diet could be the reason and will compare the numbers with Japan.

Also, there was a request to have the next version of all the application translated to Korean and other languages. John and Kate both agreed to look into having every project software go through a translation of specific languages.

It was about dinner time when Kate announced the Night Shopping, and it seemed everyone wanted to join in, so Kate told them to contact the Ambassador so arrangements could be made for extra security.

The dinner and Night Shopping was a complete success, and everyone had so much fun. Everyone went, including the press staff, and everyone got a lot of good deals. Since they are all going to be on the Leadership plane, there's going to be plenty of room to store everything and no one has to pay extra.

It was about midnight when John and Kate got back to the embassy, so they did call Jim to give him the updates. Then they called Katelin and she answered the phone in an angry voice," If you would had told me you were going to do some Night Shopping, I would have begged you to go."

John and Kate were laughing, and Kate said with one angry voice too. 'And just how did you find out about our Night Shopping?"

Katelin laughed and said," It is all over the TV. I told you that you guys are famous. Whatever you do, it will be in the news."

Kate and John were laughing too, and Kate said with a laughing voice," Don't worry honey, we bought stuff or you too. You think we have forgotten you? Your Dad is even upset because I bought more things for you than for him and myself. That's because we love you so much."

The call ended, John and Kate set their alarm for 6 am because they didn't want to miss their morning exercise before breakfast and that they should have enough time before leaving for Tokyo at 11 am.

They dozed off for the night quite happy capping their day with great food, great people and great shopping in a great place.

The Trip to Tokyo

John and Kate woke up at 6am for their exercise and also had time for a quick breakfast in the Embassy cafeteria. When they got to the cafeteria, they noticed 2 TV screens were set up, and the cafeteria was packed with people and the 2 Korean Presidents were there too to greet them, so John and Kate knew that the 2 Korean Presidents were up to something. Then the Ambassador stood up and said," This surprise is something 4 Presidents decided to do before you will leave Seoul today." Then the President of the US along with the leaders of Congress and Senate and the President of China's and some of his staff appeared on the 2 TV's.

Then the China President took over and said," After our discussion the other day. We wanted to do something that we believe will help the world. We have developed over the years a skill for building ships, and we have one that's almost completed, and we made some modifications, and we decided to donate it to be used by Doctors Without Borders. We have started to fill it with doctors, nurses and ship staff from all over the world. It will be operational this month." After that short speech, everyone cheered and since he was being televised, people all over the world were cheering for China. This is one of the significant times China did something for the world.

John and Kate nodded their heads at the President of China and smiled and John said," That's amazing, Mr. President! We are all proud of China on what they did on the medical project as well as other projects and now, this great thing will really help the world, thank you so much China."

The US President also complemented China and said," What Republic of China has done would greatly help the people of China and also the world."

The 2 Korean Presidents both stood up and thanked John and Kate for coming, shake their hands and then the President of the US said," Thanks again for everything you and your project leaders do all for the world and hope to see you home in a few days. Thank you, Mr. Ambassador, for being such a fine host. Thank you, Mr. President from China, and Mr. Presidents North and South Korea."

A loud applause once and for all echoed in the cafeteria, and people approached John and Kate to shake their hands, and when everyone had settled, they resumed eating their breakfast.

The leaders, security and the press closely monitor John and Kate as they are about to board their flight to Tokyo.

As soon as they landed in Tokyo, a big crowd of cheering people welcomed them. It's the first time for an official working for the Government that's treated like rock stars in every country that they have visited. As John and Kate stepped off the plane there were banners saying, WE LOVE JOHN AND KATE along with loud cheers. The couple responded with a big wave to the crowd and their wide smiles.

The entire team was taken to the US Embassy in Tokyo. It was around 8 pm when they finally got to their room and settled in for the night.

They called Katelin and put her on the speaker phone. Katelin was in her limo on the way to work when she answered the call and she knew it was her mom and dad, so she said," Do you know what it feels like to see your parent's faces everywhere and large crowds cheering for them? I'm one super proud daughter here."

John and Kate were laughing then Kate said," Yes, we do. I hope we always look great every time we are on camera. We know the feeling honey because we used to see your face on the front page of magazines and on large subway posters every day for several months. You were also in television beer advertisements and were famous when we lived in Japan. I can't believe you gave all that up to go to college and get a degree."

Katelin remembered the days and laughed. "When will you guys be home?"

Kate responded and said, "After our Tokyo meeting our last stop is Mexico City and then home. How are things going at work?"

Katelin answered with a sad tone," I almost had to fire a guy yesterday. As much as people were told never to lie in an expense account form, he still lied and cheated in the expense account form which amounted to about $20.00. I had to defend him from the HR people. They wanted me to fire him, but I was able to convince HR that a demotion would be enough along with a promise that he would never do it again. He was a manager, and his demotion would serve as a lesson to others to be truthful."

John consoled her," Sorry you had to go through that Katelin. I hope he realized that you fought for him, and he should be loyal to you and the others. You did good and you did the right thing." They talked for a while and then Katelin's limo arrived at her work, so they hung up.

A big day is what awaits the couple tomorrow. The first meeting is going to be a breakfast meeting with the US Ambassador and the Prime Minister at 9 am. They also will have the security audit and the project reviews. They set their alarm for 6 am and went straight to bed.

The Partnership Proposal and The Project Reviews

John and Kate woke up at exactly 6 am, got to their exercise, when done and were getting dressed to go for breakfast when there was a knock at the door. It was the butler telling them they would be meeting in a private dining area and that he would wait by the door to guide them to the area.

The couple were out within 15 minutes, and they were on their way to the dining area. When they got there the Ambassador and Prime Minister were already having their coffee and talking. When the Ambassador saw Kate and John, he got up and said with a big smile," It is so nice to see you both again. We only have to turn on our TV and we can see where you have been. The Prime Minister and I have been trying to figure out what new projects we can work on together, but both of you are experts in this area so I can't wait to hear your ideas later. Do you already have any?"

John looked at Kate and knew this was her idea, but she asked him to go ahead and discuss it with them because they are in Japan, and it would more acceptable if he would present the idea. So, John looked at the Prime Minister directly and said, "This may seem like an unusual partnership, but I think this would be very helpful to both our countries and if it works then would be helpful to the World as well."

Now the Prime Minister and Ambassador had big smiles on their faces and were on the edge of their seats as John continued, "Kate and I are always asked about Japan and how we liked living in Tokyo. We always said there is no crime. We felt very safe, including our daughter, when she goes out at night. Japan is one of the safest countries in the world. It ranks in the top 10 safest countries."

"Also, it seems like even though you sold liquor out of machines like Coca-Cola, no underage would get it. And when you go home late at night and the sign said don't walk and there was not a car in sight, no one would really cross the street. They obeyed the traffic light.

We know that a great deal of this, is taught in the family and you do not want to do things you're not supposed to, because it would embarrass your family if caught. We also believe this type of discipline was taught in Japanese schools all the way up to college. Japanese kids are one of the smartest in the world. They ranked in the top 5 smartest countries on SAT scores."

"It seems that when they go to college, they spend more of their time as young adults are there to make friends and get to know who the next Prime Minister will be. Also, find people that will help them find a job or help them once they are working. The US has the best Colleges," John boasted the thought.

"Kate and I lived here for 3 years, and she took college classes here to finish her degree.

We have also looked at statistics in this area. Now that we are in the US, it seems like we are the opposite. Some of our kids do break laws when they are young and push the boundaries when they are up to their college age. They are not rated very high when they start College.

So, your grade school kids are way above our kids and the rest of the world when they start College."

"We have graduates that are considered the smartest people in the World. So, we have the best education in the world for college students."

"So, what I propose as one of the most important partnerships we can work on together would be the Education project. Your Leadership team will put together the curriculum for all education up to college, and we will put together the curriculum for college."

"The most difficult part of all this, is to get the agreement from both our countries to accept the change in our education system. Therefore, the leaders we pick, and their team should be respected in both of our countries, and we put together case studies in small group to make sure their proposal have basis, before we implement it in the US and in Japan."

"It will take a few years before these changes could be made, but it will make our countries stronger, and the world would be a better place to live, once everyone around the world adopts this new Education system."

When John was done talking, the Prime Minister and the Ambassador were smiling and were pleased with John's proposal. The Prime Minister leaned closer to John and Kate from across the table and said loudly," I want to do it. You guys are so good. It is always a pleasure to talk with you. If we can make this happen, it will be as good as "The Medical Project'. I will bring it to my people and make the proposal and hopefully get the permission to partner with you on this Project."

John said with a smile," We will do the same thing and see if we can get an approval to proceed. Let's get this approved, to move forward and we will announce before we leave Tokyo. We will also need to assign an Education leader from the US and Japan. We can assign the Leaders when we get back to the US. Right now, the President has a Secretary of Education, and we'll have to see how both of them fit together and if they can be just one person. That person will remain in their position regardless of who the President is, so any changes will be taken care of right away."

Everyone nodded their heads in agreement, which is a custom in Japan, and everyone went to make some calls in their office before the next meeting. The Ambassador has 2 separate offices. John and Kate went into one of the offices and called Jim on his private line at home and went through the whole proposal with him. He was as excited as the Prime Minister and said,

"It's Thursday here, since we are a day behind you, I will try to get the President and the leaders of the Congress and Senate to approve so you can make the announcement before you leave."

When everyone left the room to go to the other meeting on Project reviews, it seemed like everything was a go but they both needed a few more approvals which can happen by the end of the day.

The first thing John and Kate wanted to look at was the Security Audit, so they asked Bill to present his update on the audit. When Bill got up, he looked a bit worried as he said," As you know there is very little crime in Japan as they know everyone that comes in and goes out. You must have a visa to come in and there is no way to get in since they are surrounded by water. We will leave things as they are today and not requiring a compound but as soon as there is an attempt on any leader, then a compound has to be built. I see no problem in leaving things as they are as of the moment, but they do have to change some items in their document handling which they agreed to work on this week."

John, Kate and the Prime Minister all agreed with the audit results so they moved on to the Project reviews and the first one that they would review is the Earthquake Project which they are partners with. So, the US and Japan Leader stood up and the US project leader spoke first and told everyone about the Earthquakes around the world, and that they were able to forecast if it's coming. The Japan leader told everyone about what they have done to the software to make it forecast even more in the future, so people will be made aware of the areas they should avoid building any infrastructure.

Then the other leaders got up and gave their status. It looked like everything was on schedule and everyone presented the money saved by each country in funding these projects. The Medical Project was just one example of how the cost of insurance has gone down because things are caught very early, and doctors are able to fix problems before they get worse. Also, when Medicare or Medicaid ran out of money or an increase on the cost of services, they can reduce the cost of Medicare for the elderly. The number of deaths has gone down and the quality of life is much better. The cost of Insurance has gone down because there are no storms and earthquakes, therefore the damage is less. These types of savings are found in all areas. It was a great meeting.

John, Kate, the Ambassador and the Prime Minister were all pleased with the results when they were leaving the meeting. It was around 9 pm so they checked their emails and both Japan and the US approved the Education Project and gave them permission to announce the Education Project as it was presented to them.

The ambassador said let's go to my dining area and celebrate with some Sake and discuss how we want to announce this to the World. They decided to use the same material that had been approved and will make the announcement by 9 am tomorrow and the world would be able to see it either before they went to bed, or when they wake up in the morning.

They set the time to leave at about 11am and would arrive in Mexico City at around 11pm.

The flight to Mexico takes about 12 hours, so, when they arrive it will be around midnight, and they have to rest to be able to carry on the tasks for the next day.

They sent an email announcement to everyone with the proposal that is already approved. The Ambassador set up his networks and everyone agreed to meet at 8am for breakfast, before the announcement, just in case there's any last-minute changes.

The Education System Project

John and Kate woke up an hour earlier than the alarm set. They started running around the embassy by 5 am. Breakfast is set at 8 AM with the Ambassador and the Prime Minister prior to the announcement of the newly approved project - Education Project.

After their run, they showered and prepared themselves for another day of meeting. A butler was waiting outside their door to escort them to the dining area where breakfast is served, and the announcement would be made. John and Kate sat down next to the Prime Minister, while the Ambassador savored his coffee and breakfast.

The people inside the dining hall are the Prime Minister's staff, the Ambassador's staff and his wife and all the project leaders from both US and Japan, and the Security team as well. Everyone is busy eating breakfast. John and Kate looked around and they noticed that there was a large audience, so, they guessed everyone wanted to hear about the new Education project.

At exactly 9 am, the TV cameras and lights came on and the Ambassador introduced everyone and said he was honored to have this meeting and to be a part of this new project. When he sat down there was applause.

Then when John stood up to talk, he immediately got applause from the audience. John started talking about why this project was so important. There were cheers and applause every time John finished a point. Then when Kate got up and started to talk, she applauded too.

She talked about how the process and how it should be implemented. When it was the turn of the Prime Minister, everyone went quiet while he was speaking and when he was done the applause roared inside the dining hall.

Everyone in the US, Japan and around the world knew the Education project like all the other Projects that were launched in the past would be a success. The Leadership team chose the right people to lead it.

After everything was done, the Ambassador got their cars ready to take everyone to the Leadership plane. On the way to the airport, they got a call from Jim and the President. The President told them they were working late and wanted to call them before they would leave Tokyo. They were both very pleased with the announcement and told John and Kate again that they always make America proud.

At the airport, ta crowd was still cheering for the US team. On the plane, Kate made an announcement over the PA about the Presidents call and told them to get some rest. John and Kate did give Katelin a call and Katelin shared that one of the challenges of most College students is being away from their family. "We may need more online Universities," she exclaimed. John and Kate agreed and will make it an option for some students as it may be less expensive. They ended the call like always by saying "I Love You and be careful."

The President's Meeting in Mexico

John and Kate arrive in Mexico City after midnight. Even though it was late there was still a large crowd with banners saying they loved John, Kate and the Leaders. Also, as they got off the plane there were loud cheers. John and Kate were very happy to see the crowd and waved at them as they walked down the stairs.

Their cars and security personnel were waiting for them at the bottom of the stairs. When the cars pulled up to the Embassy, a butler met them in the hallway and showed them to their room accommodation and informed them of the church service at 10 am at the cafeteria and then brunch at 11am.

They settled in to sleep for what's left of the night and did not wake up until 10 am and then they all prepared themselves for the brunch meeting. After brunch they were able to answer emails and get some work done.

The President of Mexico invited John, Kate and the Ambassador and his wife to the National Palace, which is situated on the main square of Mexico City, for a 6 pm dinner.

They showered and got dressed for church. Most of the Embassy employees were there along with the Leadership and Security team. John and Kate always pray for Katelin and each other's health and happiness. They always recall when they were young, and they were forced to go to Church by their parents. John always tells the story about him not wanting to be around his mother if he missed Sunday Mass. Now that they had gotten older, they began to really like going to Church.

After Church they stayed in the cafeteria with the Ambassador and his wife and enjoyed a great brunch. They were sitting across from each other, and Kate asked the Ambassador what he thought were the President of Mexico's biggest concerns. The Ambassador was not too sure, but he knew he was trying to grow the economy in Mexico, but he was not certain how he could make that happen. He was also concerned about all the people from Central America crossing Mexican borders.

After brunch John, Kate and the Ambassador put together the agenda for the meeting on Monday along with the US Leadership team. The Security Audit was being conducted by Bill all day Sunday, so the meeting on Monday would start at 9 am with the results of the security audit. The Project meetings would start right after that and should end at 1pm, which means they could fly home that day and be in Washington D.C. around 6 pm.

Everyone was happy when John and Kate broke the news about returning home the next day so they should pack everything tomorrow so they will be ready to leave right after the last meeting. The Ambassador was able to put out the new agenda letting the Mexican leaders and few VIPs invited at the meeting know all the changes.

The US project leaders and the Mexican project leaders met, talked and prepared for their presentations for tomorrow's meeting. John and Kate went back to their room, started packing, and then called Jim to tell him of their itineraries. They also called Katelin, put her on speaker phone and said in a very positive tone," Guess what, we are home tomorrow around 6pm. We can't wait to see you and hear your stories and what you have been doing."

Katelin laughed and said, "I guess I know what you have been doing since you and dad are in the news all the time. My life is boring compared to yours. Good luck in Mexico City and have a safe flight home."

It was around 5 pm so John and Kate went down to the Ambassador's office. His wife was sitting with him in his office so when they walked in, the Ambassador's wife stood up and hugged both of them and said,"

You guys have a lot of pull because this is the first time we have been invited to the National Palace for dinner."

John and Kate just smiled, and Kate said, "I hoped we dressed right. I guess people, like the Projects we are working on, would want to know more about us or our partners on new Projects."

The Ambassador got up from his desk and said," Okay, we better get going. We do not want to keep the President of Mexico waiting."

They all got into the limo and with security in front and behind them they headed to the National Palace. When they got there, they were ushered to the National Palace main dining room. John, Kate and the Ambassador and his wife were seated at a round table with 6 chairs.

When the President walked in with his wife, everyone stood up. He and his wife were seated right between John and Kate and the Ambassador and his wife. The President thanked them for coming and everyone greeted each other.

The President of Mexico spoke up first and asked John and Kate if they had given any thought on what Mexico and the US could partner on. Kate then said" John, the Ambassador and I talked about this a little. I believe we have something we need help on in Manufacturing. We have been working on producing climate devices for the Climate project. By the way, you could use some of the climate devices here in Mexico City. The city is in a cloud due to pollution and if we place some of these devices in strategic locations, we could clean up the air."

"John got sick one time when he was working in Mexico City, and he could barely breathe. He usually ran about 10 miles every day, and we believe it was due to the air he was breathing. If we got a good quote from Mexico to manufacture these devices, then you could be one of our main manufacturers for the world.

"The other thing we could work on as partners, is our border problem. We would need to have a faster and better way to provide VISAs for people in Central America and Mexico. You would need to stop people at your southern border unless they have a passport to get into Mexico, and if they want to get to the US, they must secure a VISA, we provide a bus service for a minimal fee with clear them at your border and off they go to the US. Their VISA would be checked before they got on the bus."

"If someone enters Mexico without you stamping their passport, then they should be detained and sent back to their country. Anyone that has a VISA can get to the US by bus. If they try to get in the US without the requirements, they will not only be detained, but they will be deported back with expenses charged to them."

Kate continued, "If you appoint a Mexican leader and the US appoints a leader from our end, then they would work together to solve the problem which may require few regulations to be changed. We will call this the Border Project."

The Mexican President looked at Kate, John and the Ambassador with a big smile and said," I want to do both of those things. We will manufacture those devices and beat any other manufacturer in the price. We will also work together to solve the border problem. Now we will celebrate this deal with some Tequila from Cozumel. What kind of Tequila do you want? We have peanut butter, chocolate, mango, etc. It is all manufacture in Cozumel, and we have any type you like," the President sounded so delighted with his offer.

John responded with a surprised look and said, "I am surprised by all the different types of Tequila, that's a lot. We will have what you are having."

Then all different types of foods were brought out with some Margaritas and different types of Tequila to taste. The dinner was outstanding. After dinner the President ask John and Kate, "When can we announce this Border Project partnership?"

Kate responded quickly and said," We will be back in the US tomorrow so let us work on the announcement and we will send you a draft this week and we can announce the Border Project, say, next week."

The President then looked at the Ambassador and said," This is why these two people are the best leaders in the World. They are great!", the Ambassador nodded in agreement.

The dinner was fabulous. After dinner on their way back to the Embassy, John, Kate and the Ambassador called Jim on the speaker phone, and they told him about the dinner and what had been initially discussed and agreed. Jim asked the couple to send him all the information on the Border project and he would get it approved by the end of day tomorrow.

When they got back to the Embassy, they set their alarm for 6 am so they could not miss their morning exercise and have some breakfast and get to their first meeting at 9am.

Mexico Project Reviews and the Trip Back Home

John and Kate woke up at 6am and completed their morning exercise and noticed that the conference room is prepped for the review Meeting. Breakfast is already served in the room, so they quickly showered and were out the door by 8 am and went to the Conference room. Their entire team were also in the conference room getting their breakfast, including the Ambassador and his wife. The room was almost full except for Mexico leadership group which was scheduled to come at 9 am and there was plenty of food for them.

John and Kate sat next to the Ambassador and his wife and just talked about the meeting yesterday with the President of Mexico. It seems he felt the same way the US felt. He did not like the caravans of people going across the country. The bus service that would take them to the border just sounded right. Also shortening the time to get a VISA to enter the US would be outstanding.

People were starting to come into the conference room and Kate noticed Bill, so she asked him if he was ready to give the results of the audit. He said he was, so Kate told him that he would be the first person on the agenda, but he still had time to have some breakfast.

Bill informed the Mexico Security leader know that they would be the first, but they had sometime for breakfast.

At 8:45am Kate stood up and welcomed everyone and told them

if they wanted some coffee or food, they still had 15 minutes and they would get started at 9am.

The Ambassador's wife and the other embassy staff that were not required to attend the meeting left after they had breakfast.

John and Kate talked with the Ambassador and told him they got a call from Jim and he told them it seemed like everyone was going to approve of the Border project. "He told us to start preparing the announcement material and the 2 President have already talked and want to move forward. They want to pass some names to you to see if you approve to be part of the project."

They decided to let everyone in this meeting know about the new partnership but would ask everyone to keep it to themselves until there is a formal announcement is made.

John and Kate assured everyone that the announcement of the new partnership could possibly be happening within the week. The leaders have to complete the selection of the people to be working for the project.

John and Kate noticed everyone was excited, so Kate stood up and briefed everyone on the Border project. She reminded everyone to keep it to themselves until the official announcement.

Then John announced the first agenda for the day, and asked Bill to give the results of the Security Audit for Mexico. They noticed that the Mexico Security leader was not there.

Bill got up and told everyone that Mexico failed the audit. Mainly because there were 2 attempts to some Mexican leaders that occurred in the past. There were security personnel and civilians killed during the incident. Mexico is highly advised to use the same security SOP of the US, that is to have a have a Compound, but the Security Leader would look into building one for compliance."

Bill then introduced the new Security leader, and the Compound would be implemented as soon as possible. The old Mexico Security Leader was found a new job. The new Mexico Security Leader decided that they would build a compound similar to the US. Everyone completed their update and Kate announced the meeting was over and everyone should go get their bags and head out to the cars to the airport. The entire US team were all excited to go home.

John and Kate went to their room and put on their traveling clothes and brought their bags to the car. The Ambassador and his wife wanted to ride to the airport with John and Kate so they could talk. The Ambassador and his wife both expressed how impressed they were of John and Kate and could understand why they are perfect to lead all of the projects. They also mentioned that they have never seen the President of Mexico so happy. He really got everything he wanted and so did the US.

When they got to the airport, another crowd of over 5000 people with signs cheering John and Kate's name and also the names of the Mexican Leaders. The press was there and got everything on TV. The Leadership plane took off with 2 Mexican Air Force planes escorting up to the US territory. It was a beautiful sight to see. The Leadership Plane headed home after a successful trip around the world.

As soon as they got into US air space 2 US Fighter jets took over and the Mexican jets went back home. They were there to make sure they got to Washington D.C. safely.

When they landed the President sent word for John and Kate, that he wanted everyone that was on this trip including the press to have dinner with him at the White House and they could bring their spouses. The pilot of the Leadership plane and the pilots of the Fighter jets were also invited.

The dinner was outstanding, and Katelin was already there because the President sent for her too and made sure she would be able to attend. The White House celebrated their safety back home and the success of their trip. Everyone was having a great time.

The President and Jim called for a meeting for John and Kate at Presidents office by 10 am to review candidates for the Border project and talk about the entire trip that they had.

When John and Kate got home, they set their alarm for 6am, said good night to Katelin and went to bed and made love.

The Border Project Review

John and Kate woke up at 6 am, back to their usual routine in the Compound which they missed so much, including breakfast at the diner in the gym. They then got into their limo at 8am so they could get to the White House one hour before the meeting with the President.

When John and Kate got to the White House, they went to the conference room and Kate started putting down some things on the whiteboard concerning candidates for the Border project as the leader.

When John and Kate lived in Tokyo, John used to run with a West Point Graduate every day. He was out of the service but had a great deal of management experience, and also had some experience with migrants and had become a lawyer defending people who came to the US. His name was Bob Durley and seemed to be a good candidate for the job. John gave him a call and got him on the phone, and they had a long conversation about the job and Bob said if he was offered the job then he would take it.

It was getting close to 10am so John and Kate went up to the Oval Office. Jim and the President were talking, and the President told his secretary to bring them in and they all sat down, and the President said, "How did you bring the migrant caravans subject up with the Mexican President?

Kate said in a serious tone," We brought up manufacturing some of our climate devices in Mexico and then he said he was tired of seeing the caravans of people going thru Mexico. We then got into a discussion of making it quicker to get a VISA to go to the US and then having a bus service with maybe a few stops in Mexico, that would take people close to the boarder in the US and from there, they can catch a bus to anywhere in the US. But before they could get on the bus, they need to show their passport to get to Mexico and their VISA if they want to be taken to the US. We think we have the ideal person for this job. We know him from our Tokyo days, and he is a West Point Graduate and a lawyer who has worked on immigration cases.

The President looked at Jim and said," These two people are amazing. They work on our biggest problems and also come up with the people and solutions. Jim and I have some people that may be able to help this person because if people want to come to the US and they are good people, we need to get them here quickly, which means we need to speed up the VISA process, and also arrange for means to get here. If they have money, it maybe by plane but if they don't then a bus service that is cheaper and safer than traveling in a caravan and then having to swim across the Rio Grande."

Jim said, "We know a few people working in the VISA department that could join the team. We also think people already working for this should report to him. Because this is a Leadership project the funding has already been approved, so he can start immediately. The Leaders in the Congress and Senate have already agreed to the new project and the funding you requested. We look at this job as being our total border and not just Mexico. Will you both be totally absorbed in the Border project, or will Bob be able to handle the bulk of the work?"

John replied in a serious tone," Like all our projects, we will have weekly meetings and then later on, we expect the leaders to take over. I have sent the announcement material to you and the President of Mexico. I suggest that if we can get both leaders approved then I am hoping that you and the President of Mexico will make a joint press conference in two days at 11 am our time and 9 am Mexico time."

Jim then suggested that we get the President of Mexico on the phone with the President, so they could discuss how they want to proceed with the announcement. The President then got his secretary and told her to set up the call as soon as possible.

John and Kate then briefed the President on the whole trip. The President and Jim were pleased with the results of the trip. As they were talking, the Presidents secretary excused and said the President of Mexico was on the line. The President did not put it on speaker phone because he wanted it to be President to President. They had a Leader of the Border project appointed and the US President said the US Leader of the Border Project will be contacting him before the announcement and they should both be standing next to them when they make the official announcement. They wanted John and Kate, as well, to be on the stage and say a few words introducing the Border project and the new project leaders from both countries.

The President was looking at John and Kate and then said" The announcement will be on Thursday. Write out how you want the meeting to go. Who will be talking and when they will be talking. I think I will start it out and then have the President of Mexico say a few words and then both of you can talk about the project and introduce the new leaders."

Also, Jim, we need to decide how Homeland Security fits into the picture. Right now, we have the Secretary of Education taking the information from the Education leader and making sure it gets implemented and maybe the Border leader should take the lead too, and then turn things over to Homeland Security to make sure it gets implemented correctly. I would ask your leaders how well my guys did implement what they requested, and if they did a good job then, rate them high but if my guys did not implement what your leaders requested then I would leave the decision to you for possible replacement."

They left the oval office as soon as the meeting ended. John and Kate called Bob Durley and told him he needs to be in Washington D.C. tomorrow as the announcement will be on Thursday at 9 am. They informed him of his salary, and the new house in the Compound that his family will stay in for security purposes. Bob agreed to everything and told them he would be in Washington D.C. tomorrow at 11 am since he was living in NY. John and Kate were excited to meet with Bob and work with him on the project.

John and Kate did some more work on the other projects and got everything set up for Bob. It was 5pm so they called Katelin to see if she wanted to meet them at Deanne's Place. She agreed, so they left work around 7 pm and met Katelin. They discussed the trip and Katelin discussed her new job. They finally got to their home in the Compound at midnight. They all went to sleep and set the alarm for 7 am.

Bob Durley – Border Project Leader

John and Kate woke up at 7 am a bit late but they were still able to complete their morning exercise and had breakfast at the new diner at the gym. They then got into the limo at 9 am so they could get to the White House one hour before the meeting with the new Border project leader.

When they got to the office, Bob Durley was already in John's office waiting for them. They almost did not recognize him. John went up to Bob and said, "Bob, have you been lifting weights? When you and I used to run in Tokyo you were a skinny guy and now you look like Sylvester Stallone," and they both laughed.

Bob just laughed and said," It comes from my training at West Point. They teach you what to eat and how to stay in shape. The running helped when I was in Tokyo but now, I have more time so increased my exercise routine."

John laughed and said, "I was in my best shape in Tokyo. Because of the food I ate, we were exercising every day. Now I have to exercise twice as much, just to maintain my weight and not gain.

"I think you have the right qualifications for this job. We want to let many people into the US, but we don't want anyone to sneak in. We do a good job at most places. When people fly in, their passport is usually checked before they board the plane, and their passport is checked again when they landed."

"The team working for the project will report to you along with the people working on the Mexican side. If someone took a flight from Spain and came into a New York airport and they did not have a passport or there was something wrong with their passport, first they probably could not board the plane but if for some reason, they got here, then they would have to be stopped."

"Based on our talk with the Mexican President, he does not want to see any more illegal caravans crossing Mexico. On our end, we do not want to see any more people coming onto our border without a valid passport. Now, we also need to make sure people can come in easily by fixing the process of getting a valid passport and VISA. These processes will be under your jurisdiction so, you will have a big job and also a lot of fixing to get it done quickly but you have everyone and everything you need to get it done."

Bob then said," Wow, indeed. Now I understand the salary and the house for me and my family, that makes sense. Let's get this announcement done so I can begin to make all this happen."

Kate butted in," We will be meeting with you and your key people around the world weekly, until you think you can have your meeting on your own. Anything that needs to be changed anywhere in the world to make this process work, just let us know."

You have the support of the President, heads of the Senate and Congress and every country around the world to make this happen, so let's make this happen."

Being a West Point graduate, Bob stood up straight to shake John and Kate's hand and said, "I will make it happen and I'm truly honored to be selected to lead this project."

John and Kate shared all the announcement materials with Bob and told him to let them know if anything needs to be changed. and not do anything until the announcement. They also let him know the current organization structure around the world and the people that will be reporting to him. He is to meet most of the people in the organization structure after the announcement and that, if he wants to make some changes, he can do it after he meets everyone.

They also discussed with him the problem of people that have overstayed their VISA or are here but are not supposed to be here. This is not a priority but as soon as he gets the first problem fixed then he can work on that problem.

After the discussion with John and Kate, he called his wife June, and told her to pack their things and move everything to the Compound house he was assigned. They were both excited and looked forward to the announcement.

John and Kate then got a status update on all the other projects and also introduced Bob to everyone as the new Border project leader. Jane was assigned to work with Bob to get things going on the project.

They also contacted the US and the Mexican President to make sure they were comfortable with their speeches and let them know about Bob Durley. Bob, John and Kate went home, and John asked Bob to join him in their limo and they would take him to his new house in the Compound.

It was a long day for everyone so they had a small dinner at their own home and set the alarm for 6 am so they could get in some exercise before the announcement at 11 am.

The Announcement of the Border Project

John and Kate woke up at 6am, had their morning exercise and breakfast at the new diner at the gym. They then got into the limo and arrived at the West Wing at 9 am.

They went to the conference room and Bob Durley was already there practicing his speech and making any changes, to fit his style. When they saw him, they went in to see if he needed any coffee since they were going to get some for themselves. He thanked them but said he was good and did not need anything.

They also let Bob know that the President would also be announcing another leader. Jen Colefarb will be joining the Leadership team as the Education leader. As they were about to talk to Bob about Jen, she entered the conference room. Jen had been an old friend from their days in Tokyo too. She spoke some Japanese and had a PHD. So, she was ideal for her new job as Education leader to partner with Japan.

Valerie entered the conference room and said everything was set up for the press conference at 11 am. The President of Mexico, the Prime Minister of Japan and the newly appointed project leaders together with the US President are all set for their press conference. Kate gave her a thumbs up and told her to let Natalie, Jim and the President know.

At 10:30 the President, Jim, Natalie and Valerie entered the conference room. John, Kate, Bob, Jane and Jen all stood up, and Kate introduced everyone and let them know how the press conference would go.

As everyone walked into the Press Conference room there was applause. This seemed to happen with John and Kate all the time. The press always knew they were in for something great.

There were 2 large TV screens in the room and when the President stepped up to the podium, he said that there would be a couple of other people joining the meeting. And the Prime Minister of Japan's name appeared on one screen followed by the name of the President of Mexico.

The US President shared the trip that John and Kate made and as a result there were 2 more partnerships that were formed. He told them about the Education and Border projects that needed to be launched. Then, he introduced the two new project leaders and asked John and Kate to talk about the 2 new projects, their partnerships with other countries and the rest of the Leadership.

John talked about the Education Project and when he sat down along with the US Leader the crowd applauded him. Then the Prime Minister introduced his education project leader and when he was done there was applause from Japan and US Press Conference rooms.

Then Kate stood up and started talking about the Border project and introduced the US Border project leader. When she was done there was applause. Then the President of Mexico introduced his Border project leader from their country, and there was applause again inside the US Press rooms.

Everyone knew these were the things that were on people's minds, and if John and Kate were involved then things would be improved. When the meeting was over the President, Jim, Natalie, Valerie, John, Kate and the 2 new project leaders left the Press Conference room that was still applauding them and went into the conference room at the West Wing.

The President then looked at everyone and said, "I guess that went well! Now we have to implement everything we talked about, but the best of the best is here so, I am confident that it will be done," as he was referring to John and Kate.

They could still hear the applause from the press Room and the West Wing as they left. Kate then spoke while looking at the 2 new project leaders and said, "I know both of you will be moving to the Compound with your families. Make sure that goes well. I also want you to make contact with the 2 new leader counterparts in Tokyo and Mexico tomorrow. That goes the same for the secretary of Education and secretary of Homeland Security and figure out how you will be interacting and corresponding with them. Start building up your teams. John and I want to meet with you every week for a while to make sure things are progressing as planned and if there are any problem we need to solve let us know immediately."

The President and Jim left the room while the others stayed inside discussing things that needed to get done. It was after 7pm when the meeting ended. John and Kate took Jen and Bob back to the compound and they continued to work from their home.

John and Kate had no meeting set up for Friday, so they did not set their alarms and planned to be at work at 9 or 10 am the next day.

The Border and Education Projects

John and Kate woke up at 7am and did their morning routine, ran, ate breakfast, prepared for work and off they went to their office at the West Wing.

When they got to their office Jen, the Education leader, and Bob, the Border project leader, were already in their office working and making calls.

John and Kate knew they picked the right individuals to lead the projects. These 2 leaders will have some of the biggest groups and may require a lot of interfacing with their team and counterparts in the US, Japan and Mexico. If the Leaders can get things right, then the US will benefit a great deal from it, and the rest of the world.

The Education system would be the best in the world by incorporating Japan's education system that is also one of the best in the world today, from primary to college years. Crime rate in Japan is very low which has a lot to do with the educational background of the Japanese students.

On the other hand, if the Border project leader can improve the VISA system which will allow more people to get VISA's faster, then, an increase on the number of people coming into the US and Mexico would be the result, as the system will make the process easier and faster. If a person has a VISA, then anyone can migrate to the US conveniently.

These two projects were the most recent projects that John and Kate initiated and wanted to give their two new leaders a week to work with the US, Mexican and Japanese governments to understand the problem and the solution. Both the Border and Education were problems the US had been working on for years with no solution.

To John and Kate's surprise the two leaders set up a meeting at the end of the day to discuss both projects. When John and Kate saw the meeting on their calendars, they knew they had picked the right people.

Bob's meeting started about 3pm and he outlined a VISA system which was much shorter in timeline than it used to be. It would outline why getting a VISA would be much faster and better for a person to get a VISA than travel across Mexico and cross the border illegally. When this new system gets published then everyone would focus on getting a VISA rather than making a long trip which could end up getting them detained and deported. He was working with his team so he could publish and announce the new process in one month.

Jen's meeting started right after Bob's. She was able to get the Japanese curricula and review it with the people in the US. The US people were going to get back to her in a couple of weeks to let her know how it fits. The Japanese has made plans to travel to some of the best US Universities and will be seeing what they can bring back to Japan.

Japan was looking for university leaders to see if they could collaborate with Japan to help them improve or modify some of Japan's universities. This would be an assignment where they would pay for their temporary move to Japan with their family. They would also pay them the regular salary plus an additional amount if they had to move to a city that was more expensive like Tokyo. They would also pay for their children's education in an American School in Japan plus any expenses that they may have while attending the academic program. If they had their children in College then they would pay for their trips when they are on break from college. They would also pay for the extra room so they had a place to stay when the visited their parents.

The US agreed to a similar arrangement with exchange student for grade school leaders coming from Japan to the US. They will put the curricula together for all educational levels. They would help make the curricula in the US similar to that in Japan.

John and Kate were very pleased with both meetings and were also pleased with all the other Project Leaders who they met after lunch. Everything was going well so now John and Kate were ready to introduce some new projects but had not set the date for these announcements, but they plan to do it soon.

The Project Challenges

John and Kate woke up at 10 am since they did not set any alarms for today because it's Saturday. They did not have to go to work or make any work calls.

Katelin had sold her house and moved into her parents' home that was in the Compound provided by the government for security reasons. Kate went up to her door and knocked. Katelin was still in bed and was still asleep, so Kate woke her up and said, "We have not seen you in a long time, so we want to have breakfast together."

Katelin smiled and said, "I had a busy week and I appreciate you letting me sleep until 10:30. This is getting a little crazy. I am a board member of my company and I still live with my parents. I know it is for safety reasons. I wonder if they have a small house in the compound that I can move into? What are we going to do today?"

Kate smiled and said, "You know your dad and I love the idea of you staying with us, but we understand you wanting your own place. We talked with Jim, and he said he is getting other requests from other leaders about their adult children, so he is looking into building smaller homes in the Compound. For now, it is not safe to live outside the compound even if they put extra security on you."

"As for the things we plan to do today, we were thinking of getting our breakfast first here in the compound and then watching a movie. Do you want to do all this with us? Or do you have any plans for today? What about some shopping?" Kate gave her a wink.

Katelin replied with a smile, "Yes count me in if I can bring Jeff Albright. We need to do some fun things and I guess we will be safe with my security and your security."

Kate was surprised, "Why Jeff? I thought you were going out with the doctor?"

Katelin said with a smile, "I really like my freedom. My doctor friend is busy today with a couple of surgeries, so I called Jeff to see if he was busy and he's not, so we both are free and we can just spend a relaxing day together, with the both of you I guess."

Kate said, "I am fine with either guy. I will let your dad and security know our plans for today."

When Kate told John that Katelin would be joining them and bringing Jeff Albright, John replied with a smile and said, "Great, he is super smart and I would like to see some of the new things we are doing on the Medical Project. Also, he will learn a thing or two from us."

Everyone got dressed and let security know that Jeff would be meeting them at the diner in the gym for breakfast and also told them about their entire plan for the day including the movie. The diner at the gym was about a mile from their house but they decided to take the car there since it was hot outside, and they were going to need the car to go to the movie.

When they arrived, Jeff was sitting at a table for four people. Security was posting nearby the table close to the door with a total view of everyone. When John, Kate and Katelin walked in, the owner greeted them and showed them to their table. Jeff stood up and greeted Katelin and pulled back her chair and said, "Nice to see you again Mr. and Mrs. Columbo and thank you for inviting me, as he greeted them with his sweet smile."

Katelin smiled and said, "It is good to see you again too. I wanted to see how you were doing on The Medical Project. How are things coming along?"

John and Kate leaned in to hear what Jeff was going to say. They know the Medical Project was going well from a high level. Death records were down and everyone in the world was using the Application, but they did not know the details of the programming and the new work that was being done to improve the project.

Jeff responded with a great deal of enthusiasm, "I was sent to a University in Morgantown, West Virginia to look at what they were doing with wearables. We are working with a company and also at a university to look for a watch that can communicate with the main frame computer. Many watches can communicate with your iPhone but we need the information in our main frame so we can make decisions on the data."

"Paul has put me in charge of taking all the information off the watch and iPhone and briefing the person wearing the watch. Right now, everything is limited to West Virginia, but we want to expand that application worldwide."

John and Kate, were so interested in this topic and Paul, Jeff's boss, knew this since John and Kate were talking about having wearables that would be able to communicate with mainframes since their college days when John and Paul were taking many of the same classes until John went off to become an Aerospace Engineer and Paul became a psychiatrist, which, John and Kate later convinced to being the Project leader of the Medical Project.

John asked Jeff, "When Paul and I talked about people being able to get direct information from the medical computer based a problem in their body detected by a wearable and then informed to stop doing or even start doing something which may help them prevent an illness we were thinking the programming involve would be very difficult. Were you able to make that happen?"

Jeff then pointed to the diner's door, and Paul Darma, the Leader of the Medical project, was about to join them for breakfast.

He was the best man at John and Kate's wedding and lives in the Compound now. Jeff said with a smile on his face, "Paul is one of the best managers I have ever had. When I told him that I would be having breakfast with the 3 of you, he knew it would turn into a discussion about the work we are all doing. He knew exactly when to show up."

Now everyone at the table was laughing and even Paul standing at the door of the diner holding out his arms waving at them.

The security team knew Paul. John, Kate and Katelin all motioned for Paul to come over to their table and John said, "Get that chair over at the table and bring it over here and sit down and join us. You were the best man at our wedding, you are our best friend, and you are leading one of the most important Projects in the world. You and your team are known all over the world. Your team has saved so many lives. I guess we don't say it enough, but I hope you and your team see it when you travel around the world. Everyone we meet with has someone in their family or someone they know that has been saved by the Medical Project," John said proudly.

Paul then said with a very proud look on his face, "Jeff and everyone on our team know how the Medical Project is helping people because before the day starts, we put out a short email with the latest numbers concerning lives saved. What Jeff and the team does not know is some of the story about John one of our leaders." Paul knew everything about John and Kate, so he wanted everyone to know a little story about John, so he continued and said, "John and I used to communicate all the time when we were young. John was doing Artificial Intelligence (AI) programming before it was known. When he was a young Engineer, he was one of the few that was also trained in programming. He was asked to put together a software package that could be sold worldwide that would be able to predict when power go beyond a certain point so they could begin to shut things off, so the power would stay below a certain limit, and this would keep the power bill at a minimum. He did this by looking at patterns or history because you had to shut down things long before you reached the peak of power."

"When John and Kate talk about AI in the Medical Industry, they are telling us if you do these things based on history or is it from reality. For example, we are very close to using AI to tell a person based on their history, if they continue to do these things then this is what will happen so they can make the decision themselves to stop doing certain things if they don't want something not good to happen to them. This is just taking what John was doing only using it in the Medical Industry and calling it AI."

This was a story about John that no one knew about at the table, except John and Paul. John, with a smile on his face looked at Paul and said, "Thank you Paul, you are such a great friend, and you really know our history together. We both know that you, Jeff and the rest of your team have taken this AI in the Medical Project to a higher level. You are also working with universities that has Programmers, Engineers, Medical Doctors and business-minded people that can continue to build what we started. I know you and Jeff are working with universities and companies to take the Medical Project to the next level. Kate and I are really proud of the Medical Project team. Also, we need to thank Katelin for introducing Jeff to the team."

Katelin looked at her dad and Paul with a proud look on her face," I guess I am going to have to invite Paul to a few more meetings. Every time Paul is with us, I find out more about dad's younger days and the things he did. Makes me prouder of him than ever."

Kate also said with a smile on her face, "I want to thank you both, Jeff and Paul for joining us this morning. Because of your team and the success of the Medical Project we are being trusted with many more projects. Now, more countries around the world would want to partner with the US on any special projects that can help their country. We want you to keep up the good work and if there is anything you need, just reach out to us and we will make it happen."

At this moment John, Katelin and I were going to go to a movie at the mall and then do some shopping. You are both welcome to join us." as Kate gave them her sweet smile.

Jeff and Paul declined for the movie because they both had some work they wanted to complete on the Medical Project and the wearables. John, Kate and Katelin needed the break from their jobs, so they got into the car and went off to watch a movie.

Paul and Jeff had some ideas they wanted to explore after talking with John and Kate, so they went to the West Wing to do some more work on the Medical Project after their breakfast.

After the movie and shopping John, Kate and Katelin were tired so they decided to go home and do some work at home and then go to bed early so they could go to an early mass tomorrow.

The Big Covid Problem in Brazil

John and Kate were so used to waking up early that they woke up at 7:30 and decided to go to the 8:30 mass and then do some exercise after the mass. Katelin said she would join them. They let security know their plans to go to the 8:30 mass and then come home and exercise for about couple of hours. No work, no calls, no emails, just Sunday. And for their security they had 4 guards follow them to church and back.

Church went well. They each prayed for each other's safety and good health and so far, that has been working. Kate always said they had the best guardian angels. When they got back to the Compound, they did their 2.5 hours of exercise together and then they relaxed in their yard. They were not talking but just sitting and looking up at the blue sky.

After about a half hour of relaxing, John's phone rang and before John answer the phone Kate said, "I knew this was too good to last."

John had a serious look on his face as he answered the phone and looked at Kate and said, "It is from Paul Darma." Then he answered the phone saying, "Hello Paul, why are you calling?"

Paul replied in an urgent voice, "I hate to bother you on a Sunday, but the Medical program gave us an alert. It appears to be an area in Brazil with more than 1000 people were having a high fever and a low oxygen level in their blood, plus some other negative symptoms within a one-mile radius in Rio De Janeiro, Brazil.

Because we had agreements with everyone in the world that if anything like this happened then we would lock down the area until we could find a cure. John and Kate immediately got Jim and the President on the phone so they could call the President of Brazil. The President of Brazil then locked down all travel in and out of Rio De Janeiro. The Medical Computer also put out an automatic message so everyone including the press would be alerted to the information.

John and Kate flipped a coin to see which one of them would be flying to Rio. Kate won the toss so she would be going. They decided that a predetermined team of doctors from all over the world that were experts on Covid, and different viruses would be going. Paul Darma and Jean Meadows would also be joining Kate on this trip. The plan was to leave Sunday at midnight so they would be there first thing Monday morning.

So, this new virus would not spread outside of Rio as the whole city was locked down where the 1000 people were located. It was in an area that came alive every Sunday. People would come in from all over Brazil and the streets were shut down to cars and people would walk on as they shop on the streets. It was the Ipanema and Copacabana Beach area.

The President of Brazil had shut down all streets leading into and out of that area of Rio. The police were all over the city, and all airports with planes flying into Rio were cancelled. It's Standard Operating Procedure(SOP) that was being implemented as soon as the computer detected the virus. The only good thing is that this area of Rio has a lot of nice hotels and restaurants where people can stay and eat until the doctors arrive and a cure is found. Also, there were some hospitals in the area and tents were being erected for triage on the beaches of Ipanema and Copacabana since the hospitals were filled to capacity.

John and Kate left Katelin at home, and they went to their office at the West Wing and work until the problem stabilized. If she had any emergency to just call them. They would always keep their cell phone close to them, and it is always on. Kate would be flying out tonight while John would be around with Katelin.

When John and Kate got to the West Wing, Paul Darma and his whole team were there on the phones and computers. Paul met with John and Kate and talked about the issue, "The number of people with the new virus had grown since the last report, from 1000 to 1500 people. The good news is that it is still contained within the Ipanema and Copacabana area. Our doctors here were able to reproduce the virus and have found a vaccine to kill it without harming the person.

"The Leadership plane is being prepared to fly to Rio tonight at 11pm with masks, equipment, vaccines and doctors. Our doctors are constantly in communication with the doctors in Rio so they will know what they need to bring and also what type of virus we are dealing with. We know it is very contagious and two hundred people have died. They believe they have an idea what type of virus it is and hopefully with the vaccines it would knock this thing out before it spreads."

The Leadership plane was full to capacity when it took off and everyone that boarded the plane was given the vaccine shot. When the Leadership Plane landed at the airport close to Rio there were thousands of people and press cheering at them. John got Kate and Paul on a speaker phone and told them the number of people with the virus was up to 2000 and 400 fatalities as for the latest update.

There were 10 large buses that brought all the people and supplies to the main headquarters for the vaccine operation in Rio. There were people cheering as the buses drove down the highway to Rio. When they arrived at the hospital doctors, nurses, press and families of the sick ones looked at them hoping that they could make the virus go away at once. The doctors and nurses immediately started administering the vaccine.

Kate, Paul, Jean and all the doctors and nurses they brought with them worked all day and night. It was a miracle. The number of people with the virus started going down and the number of deaths stayed at 400.

Everything worked the way they had expected since the alert, to the lock down, to the development of the vaccine and then the virus was eliminated. The Medical Project and Kate's team stopped Covid from spreading and claiming more lives in Rio. So, the medical project team did not stay any longer, when they had mitigated the virus and gradually eliminated it, they flew back to the US.

When the Leadership Plane landed people were cheering at them at the airport. The White House provided buses that would take everyone including the pilots to the White House. There was a huge banquet prepared for them with the press invited to cover another success story. There were several speakers and entertainers as well. A great time to celebrate for America.

At the end of the banquet, the President gave an official statement and asked the audience. "What do you think this Leadership team will do next?"

On the way home, Kate told John, "I guess now is the time to talk about our next project since the President was wondering what we would do next."

John just smiled and said, "I guess that is why I married you. You never stop and you keep us going all the time. Should we introduce everyone to our new interplanetary Blackhole Spacecraft?"

Kate just looked at John and smiled. They went back to their home in the compound made love and went to bed. They set the alarm for 6:30am so they could get in their exercise and then meet with the US President and Jim which they told Valerie to set up at 10am to discuss the next project.

The Black Hole Starship

John and Kate woke up at 6:30am and nothing extraordinary for today, as they do their morning exercise and breakfast routine, except that they were excited to talk with Jim and the President at 10 am about the new Black Hole Propulsion System Project that they will propose. When they stopped at the breakfast Diner at the gym they started their discussion about the project.

They knew the magnets would help in getting the space station out of our atmosphere and to the moon, but as you increase the distance between magnets the speed slows down. That is when they needed to come up with something like you would see in Star Trek movies where the pilot pulls a lever, and the spacecraft moves very fast.

This will allow the big space station to get to Mars or any place in space quickly. John and Kate have created a Black Hole Propulsion system capable of interstellar travel using a black hole as an energy source for spacecraft propulsion. They have done some testing of the Black Hole Spaceship propulsion for a few minutes when traveling to the moon and also in the lab but now they were ready to announce it to the world and also use it in the trip they are planning to Mars.

John had drawn a small sketch on a napkin. It showed the details on how the Black Hole Propulsion system would work and then John said with a very serious tone to Kate, "I know we will not be able to describe the Black Hole Propulsion system in this detail to the President, Jim or the press using this," holding the napkin in his hand. "I will just tell them we have invented a new Black Hole Propulsion System which will get us places faster than ever before. We can let them know we are working with a University in West Virginia and no one other than the President, Jim, 5 people at the University, the Space Project Leader, and the two of us who knew the details of this propulsion system. The team at West Virginia is going to Switzerland's particle collider to get the black holes from the particle collider and we have another company designing the other parts of the system along with the programming needed to make the system work."

Kate added," We want to get everyone's approval to move ahead with this project and also decide how and when we want to announce this. Should we bring in any partners? We will see how the President and Jim would want to proceed when we meet them later. It is 8 o'clock so we better head home and get ready to meet them," and they went back home, got dressed and off they went to their meeting place.

John and Kate were at the West Wing at 9:30 and went to Jim's office. With a very serious look Jim said, "This meeting will be in the Oval Office, so we better start going there now."

On the walk to the Oval Office, John and Kate briefed Jim on the new propulsion system. Jim was smiling the whole time while listening.

When they reached the Oval Office and was let in by the secretary, they noticed the President invited some members of the Congress and the Senate. He stood up as soon as he had seen them coming and said," Ah, there you are. My three favorite people. Since I know you will be asking approval to proceed with a new project, I thought it would be best to have everyone that needs to approve it here in the Oval Office."

Everyone then sat down around the table and was served coffee. The President then said, "We have not turned down any of your projects and all of them have been very successful. We are all very excited to hear about this project. "

John and Kate then describe the whole project as they discussed it in Diner this morning. Everyone reacted with excitement when they heard the details of the project. There was applause as they listened.

Then at the end Kate said with a very serious tone, "Since we used Russia and China as partners on the Space project, we were thinking of using them again and opening it up to any other partners as long as the people in this room approve along with Russia and China."

The President then smiled and said, "That is why you guys are the best. Not only did you and your team come up with a great invention you are also looking how the rest of the world will benefit and we will not have people afraid of what we will do with this invention."

John added," We will open it up to the world. We had a contest to see who could build the best Mars Land Rover and West Virginia University won so that is the Land Rover we will use. There are a few other things we will need to see what countries and companies will submit their item and compete. Whoever wins, will become one of our official partners for this project."

Everyone agreed and then the President said "We will announce the Black Hole Starship on Monday which will give you time to come up with the way you want to announce everything including the contest guidelines for the partnership. It will also give you time to contact Russia and China and asked if they want to be our partner and also get their input on the announcement."

Everyone agreed to meet on Friday again, after John and Kate polished all the details to discuss it with Russia and China's technical leaders. When John and Kate went back to their office, she asked Valerie to set up calls tomorrow with Andrei the Russian leader and the China Secretary General.

John and Kate then got the US Space Project leaders and started putting together how and what the announcement would look like and the important points they should discuss with Russia and China.

Their meeting ended at about 9pm and Valerie let everyone know that Russia and China would meet at 9am and 10am US time on Thursday.

John and Kate confirmed with everyone their meeting meet tomorrow morning at 8am to discuss the final charts they would use.

Then they went home, had a quick dinner with Katelin who was staying with them that night and then went to bed.

The Launching of the Black Hole Starship Project

John and Kate woke up at 6:00 am with excitement and anxiety for the discussion that they will have with Russia and China about the new Black Hole Propulsion System Project. They still manage to complete their routine, stopped at the diner and polished on the discussion on what output they wanted to get out of the meetings with Russia and China.

Kate suggested in a very serious tone, "We should offer Russia and China the opportunity to have astronauts on the Black Hole Starship. We can ask them to build parts of the Black Hole Starship per our specifications like they did with our Space Station. Then we should see if they wouldn't mind having Switzerland or other countries that would want to be partners in this project."

"The Black Hole Starship we have designed is similar to the Spaceships we saw on the TV show Star Trek. It will hold more than 20 people and have bedrooms, cafeterias, propulsion rooms and also have enough food and oxygen to last a lifetime. People will be able to walk around the Starship similar to how they did in the Space Station and also the Spaceship on the TV show."

"We will leave the earth's atmosphere using our magnets similar to how we went to the moon but once we are in space, we will activate the Black Hole Propulsion system which will allow us to travel quickly and faster in space. It should only take a day to get to Mars."

John then responded to Kate with a smile and said," I agree with everything you said. We better run back home and get to the first meeting at 9 am."

John and Kate were able to get to the conference room just in time for the zoom call that was just being set up. The US Space leader was there, and Valerie was getting everyone connected in Russia. The call started at 9 am US time and they noticed the US Ambassador to Russia was in the room with Andre and the Russian Space leader.

Everyone could see each other on the call. Since everyone knew each other already, Andre started by saying. "John and Kate, it is so nice to see you again and I understand there is another Space Project you want us to be your partner. Before you even tell us what it is, I can say that I already talked with my President, and we are both going to say Yes. We trust you so much and you have done so much for Russia and the world that we don't want to miss this very opportunity. We always want to be your project partner. But please tell us what this project is and how we can be of help."

John then started to discuss the details and description of the project, its scope and main objective just as he discussed it with Kate. As John described the project, Andre was simply amazed and immediately gave his comment, "You two have done it again. I will discuss with the President of Russia, and I am sure he would approve on being your partner on this one. What would you want us to do?"

Kate then started talking and described what Russia would do, and she presented the idea that Russia and China would build the Black Hole Starship following and using their specifications. They will also each supply 2 astronauts. Then she said in a questioning tone, "Since we were getting a lot of support from Switzerland in building the black holes, we were thinking of adding them as a partner and also ask them to supply 2 astronauts. We have also been working with Japan and South Korea on AI Robots. Would you be ok with adding Switzerland and other partners like South Korea and Japan to the Space project if they can add value?"

"I believe both of you are fantastic," Andre said and went on to say. "Before we set up ground rules for adding partners you included Russia and China as partners that must agree on the partner. I am fine with Switzerland, Japan or South Korea being partners as long as you said they add value. I also believe that our 3 countries have to agree before a partner is added. We are also making Robots and so is the US. China and Hong Kong invented a robot called Sophia. So, I will get back to you later today to make sure that first, our President agrees with me and wants to be your partner on this, and second, he would agree on adding other partners that can add value to this project."

The US Ambassador to Russia then spoke up and said, "Again it is an honor for me to be in this room and hear about this fantastic project. I hope Andre can get the approval on everything. Also, I will assume until everyone gets their approval on everything, that we should not discuss this with anyone and will treat this with utmost confidentiality. Additionally, I assume there will be a joint announcement. When do you think the announcement will take place?"

John then said with an agreeable tone, "You are correct Mr. Ambassador. We should not make any announcements until all partners have agreed on everything that's been laid out on this project. At the moment, we need to get a timetable for when the Starship will be completed. We also need to get some AI Robots that will be used to test the Starship. We will need to announce our partners to the world and what the partners will be doing. We will create the timeline for the test schedule and when the actual launch to Mars will take place."

The meeting ended and everyone agreed to get together at the same time tomorrow after Andre had a chance to talk and get their President's response and approval. As soon as that meeting ended, they prepared for the next zoom call meeting with China.

Appearing on the zoom call from China was the Secretary General and the China Space Project leader, and a couple of astronauts from the mission to the moon. It almost started out the same way as the

Russian meeting with the Secretary General saying, "I understand this is a meeting to see if we want to be a partner in your next project? My President and I already discussed this when the moon project was launched, and we decided we would always want to be your Partner in any Project you propose. But I guess I need to hear it and bring it to my President to officially get his approval on this Project."

John and Kate went through the complete details of the project, with everyone from China. They also then described the additional partners and rules for adding any other possible and interested partner. They agreed that China, Russia and the US all have to approve should there be a new partner."

The Secretary General was amazed at the idea about traveling to Mars, and he said with a great smile, "You two are simply amazing. This is something that amazes me and I am sure will amaze the world as well. Of course, we want to be your partner, but I will verify with our President and get back to you tomorrow. Asfar as other partners, you know we have the Robot called Sophia which was built in Hong Kong. I understand Japan and South Korea lead in the AI Robot business. I also know the US has some fantastic AI Robots they use today in the Medical Industry."

"You are asking Russia and China to build the Starship so maybe we need to share the expenses and find the best robot we can use. Maybe we will need more than one type of robot depending on the task we ask them to do. I will get back to you tomorrow at this time with our formal answer."

When the call ended, Valerie suggested that they need to have a meeting with Jim. Jim agreed to have a lunch meeting with them and the President at noon at the White House dining area. When they looked at their watches, they noticed it was due to start in half an hour.

John and Kate took a break and then met in Jim's office, and they all walked to the dining area and while they were walking, they briefed Jim on what they were going to tell the President. As they were walking Jim's smile got wider until he could not hold back and said,

"It is hard enough to get our own government to agree on something and you do that well, but you also have the trust of the world, so they also agree on everything you propose. I am sure the President is going to feel the same way."

When they got to the dining room the President welcomed them again with a big smile on his face and said, "My three favorite people. You would not believe who I have been talking to this morning. If you guessed the Presidents of China and Russia, then you would be correct." He stopped for a moment and then said, "Let me tell you a story, "Every manager and leader have one person if they are lucky, to send to any meeting and after the meeting is over, they will either get an email or phone call saying how great that person was in the meeting. We are lucky we have both of you that we can send to any meeting and get calls and emails saying how good the person is. That goes for the both of you."

Then he stopped for a few seconds and continued," The first call was from the Russian President thanking me for including Russia in this project as a partner. He actually asked me jokingly if I was sure if both of you were Americans. He believes you are both Russians or your mothers and fathers were Russians. He then said maybe there are some people we need to say they are from this world and not any particular country because you do help the world. That is a huge complement coming from the Russian President. He then said as far as adding partners he liked the idea of getting agreement from Russia, China and the US before any partner is added and they must add value to the partnership we have today."

"Then I got a call from the China President, and he was almost laughing in his own words saying, 'This Project is fantastic, John and Kate are fantastic, of course we want to be your partner,' "as he mimics how the President from China said it.

"When we announce this project to the World, then everyone will be as amazed as we are today. I like the idea of other partners which can reduce the cost that each country will need to spend. We have agreed to build the Starship with the US, China and Russia. The cost of some of the AI Robots are over a million dollars each. I am okay with any of the partners mentioned. I think your meeting tomorrow will have good results."

John and Kate went back to their office and took care of some business and had Valerie confirm the meeting tomorrow with Russia and China again. She also had her call Katelin to set up a dinner with her at Deanne's. They also invited Jean Meadows and the Space Project leader to dinner but asked them if they could arrive an hour earlier before Katelin does, so they could bring up to speed everything that's covered in all of the meetings.

Jean, the Space Project leader, John and Kate all arrived at Deanne's restaurant at 6pm and sat at table for 5 in a private room in the restaurant. Kate started the meeting by telling everyone in a very serious tone, "It looks like we are going to Mars. John and I would like the first Starship going to Mars to be run by robots since we really need to test a lot of things on the Starship, and it will be the first time we use the Blackhole Propulsion System. The plan will be to have the robots take the ship out of our atmosphere using magnets and then engage the Black Hole Propulsion System which will get the Starship to Mars in one day. We will land a Space Station with a robot on Mars. That robot will use parts on that Space Station to build a bigger Space Station on Mars and will stay there until another crew lands on Mars next to that Space Station the robot has built. The Robot we will leave there is atomic powered and only gets energy from the sun. The robot will be able to live there for more than 100 years.

"If everything goes well on Mars, then we will bring it back to the Starship circling Mars by engaging the Black Hole Propulsion System to take 1 day to come back to earth."

"Then we will land the Starship using magnets. If this all works, then 2 weeks later we will do this same trip with astronauts and will leave another Space Station on Mars with another robot staying at the Space Station. Those robots will be able to conduct many tests and be able to walk and ride the Mars Land Rover all around the planet. The Robots don't need food or oxygen and will use the sun to power themselves. Also, the Space Station on Mars will power itself using the sun and nuclear power for 100 years."

John then said, "We were able to pick the Mars Land Rover by having a competition. I believe it would be great Jean if you could run a competition and get your counterparts in Russia and China to judge which country had the best robots for a certain task. I think we will need several robots. You should include Japan, US, China and South Korea in the competition. Those are the countries we believe have the best AI Robots but there may be other countries that want to be included in the competition, so let's keep it open to all. We will also need another robot that stays and operates the Space Station on Mars."

Kate then spotted Katelin coming to the table, so she waved to her and said, "We were just ending a meeting. You should join us."

Since Katelin was one of the board members of her company, she had 4 security people with her, and they sat at a table along with John and Kate's security people. Before she sat down Jean said to Kate, "You and Katelin are really close. How did you get so close?"

John said with a serious tone, "The moment Katelin was born, Kate knew she had a friend and daughter for life. I am just a lucky guy to have two beautiful smart people that love me. My daughter may respect me, but she loves her mother. They talk or email each other every day. They are that close," as he both gave a wink to Kate and Katelin.

Katelin smiled as she sat down, "Are you two talking about me again." The waiter came to the table and Katelin said with a big smile, "I will have the same things these guys are having. It seems like they are having a good time." Then Katelin turned to everyone at the table and said, "Don't worry, I do have top secret clearance and I will divulge anything whatever it is you talked about at this table."

Kate then said in a serious tone, "We are all done discussing our business and you will probably read about it in the paper in a couple of weeks. Let's just enjoy the food." And everyone started to eat and enjoyed the food that's served.

After dinner was over, everyone went home. John and Kate set their alarms for 6am so they could get in their exercise and get to their meetings with Russia and China for their second round of space project discussion.

The Robots and the Black Hole Starship

John and Kate woke up at 6:00am and have their exercise and were excited to talk with Russia and China so they can begin the testing of the Starship and the selection of the AI Robots. They wanted to talk with Russia and China about the mission to Mars with the AI Robots.

Valerie got Russia, China, the Space leaders, John and Kate on a call. John started out by saying, "At first we thought we should not send Astronauts to Mars but now we believe it will be safe enough to use Astronauts from the 3 countries. We will also use AI robots, test them out and leave one of the AI Robots on Mars so we can monitor the testing and start building a big Space Station there. When it's completed, then everyone can come back to Earth."

"We will announce this mission tomorrow if everyone agrees and then plan to leave in one week, if we can get everything ready. The plan will be to have one Starship with 9 astronauts, 6 from Russia, China and the US. Two from each Country. We will also bring 3 astronauts from Switzerland, Japan and South Korea. One from each Country. There will also be 6 AI robots."

"We plan to have the astronauts engage if they see the AI robot having a problem because on the next mission, we will be asking the AI Robots to take on bigger tasks if they do well on this trip."

When John finished his discussion, everyone agreed, and John distributed the copies for tomorrow's announcement materials and asked everyone if there were any changes they thought they needed to make, they had to send it to him first thing in the morning.

After the meeting John and Kate briefed the President and Jim. They also let them know that all the Astronauts were feeling fine so they will not have to make this trip.

John and Kate then called Katelin and asked her to meet them for dinner at Deanne's Place. Before they left work, they made sure all the testing was being performed on the new Starship and also the AI robots that would be on the Starship. The 9 astronauts were due to arrive tomorrow to resume testing.

When John and Kate arrived, they noticed that there was extra security at the restaurant and then saw at a round table at the back of the room the President, Jim, their wives and Katelin all at the same table with 2 empty seats.

The President stood up when John and Kate arrived at the table, and said as everyone got seated, "These things that you both have done and continue to do have allowed our world to be more trusting of each other. Maybe this is because they know we have become again the leader in the world, and they trust us so much. You two have become the most loved and trusted people here on Earth."

"We know that both of you will become very busy over the next few months, so we wanted to take this time to get together and thank you for a job well done."

When John and Kate got home, they made love. John always thought he was lucky to have such a beautiful person that loved him. He never cheated on Kate and always knew she had his back and loved him. As John and Kate stayed close through the years, Kate looked more beautiful to John each day.

They set the alarm so they could get up and get ready for the big announcement about the trip to Mars.

As John was looking at his calendar before he shut his eyes, he noticed that Kate had a doctor's appointment. It was for a colonoscopy at a clinic as an outpatient. It was in the afternoon, so John woke Kate up just as she was about to close her eyes and asked her about the appointment, they made a month ago and she had been putting it off, but John insisted they go, and she agreed.

The Black Hole Starships and the Cancer

John and Kate woke up at 6 am and were eager to complete their exercise so they can get ready and make the announcement to the Russians and Chinese about the trip to Mars. They arrived at the West Wing, stopped by Jim's office and the 3 of them went to the press room together. When they arrived the 9 astronauts and the Space leaders from all the countries were already in the call.

As they were announcing everything there was constant applause. John and Kate also announced the second mission to Series and Proxima Centauri if the Mars mission went well. John and Kate were going to announce the next Space endeavor but decided to wait for another day. When they left the press room they were still cheering.

That afternoon they went to Kate's scheduled colonoscopy. John noticed as he was waiting for it to be completed, what usually takes an hour laboratory exam took more than two hours. The doctor came out and told John he found cancer in Kate's colon, and they need to make an appointment with a colorectal surgeon as soon as possible.

John was aghast, when he went in to see Kate as she was waking up from the anesthesia, the doctor stayed in the room with them and informed the couple that she may have to wear a bag for the rest of her life. They took the news sadly, and Kate urged John to go home and discuss the matter with him privately.

When they got home Kate told John she didn't want to have surgery. John could not change her mind so he thought he would call Nancy, who was Jim's wife who he had worked for, and he knew Kate respected her and told her of the situation.

Nancy talked it out with Kate and convinced her to get the surgery, and promised she would be there for her during the surgery. This was the best time for John and Kate to use the medical computer and find the best surgeon. They found a doctor at the Mayo Clinic in Jacksonville that was the best and they talked with him and sent him the results of the colonoscopy and said he could do the surgery and she would not have to wear a bag all her life.

They made the appointment to have the surgery as soon as they could. They had an opening on Monday, so John let Nancy know and they all made plans to be in Jacksonville on Monday for the surgery.

John told the US Space Leader and Jean the Project Office leader; they would have to oversee all the tests and make sure it's done because they would not be around on that day.

During the whole week, there was more testing done than ever before. Since they would be using AI robots for most of this trip. The Starship needed to be tested and each of the AI robots needed to go through a great deal of tests.

On Wednesday everyone would be ready for the launch to Mars. The systems were completely tested, and they have all the data needed for their trip to Mars.

Kate's Surgery

John, Kate and Nancy all made arrangements to be in Jacksonville since Sunday to prepare for the surgery. John and Kate went to the church on Saturday to get a blessing from the priest. They asked Kate to check into the hospital by Sunday in preparation for the surgery.

On Monday Nancy was there for John and Kate at the hospital. There was a TV that would show when Kate went in for surgery and when the surgery began until it ended. The surgery was about 7 hours. During that time Nancy was there for John. They went to lunch, and they went to the gift shop and got a teddy bear they called Mayo, for the Mayo Clinic.

After the surgery, the doctor came out to talk with John and Nancy. When he told John he got all the cancer, and she would have to wear a bag for one month so the area of the colon they had removed could heal.

John just kept thanking the doctor. He told him he did something other doctors said could not be done without wearing a bag her whole life. The Medical computer recommended using this doctor and the medical computer was right.

Nancy and John slept with Kate in her private room in the hospital. A few times when Kate was in a great deal of pain, Nancy and John pleaded with the doctors to give Kate more pain reliever medicine.

Kate asked John to help her with the emptying and changing of the bag and was happy he would only have to do that for one month. She encouraged him to be there for Starship launch to Mars. He said he would make sure everything would go well.

Every time the doctor came in John called him a great doctor. The doctor just said that it was just plumbing. John just laughed and kept praising the doctor for the good job that he did with Kate. He was able to get all the cancer and she would only have to wear a bag for one month. Everyone was happy.

The Trip to Mars, Series and Proxima Centauri using AI Robots and Black Hole Starships

John woke up at 6 am at the hospital and did a little exercise just to energize him and was fetched by helicopter to Washington D.C. and then to the command room at the White House to get ready for the launch.

Nancy stayed with Kate and made sure Kate was taken care of. When the hospital asked Kate how they were related. Kate and Nancy just laughed. They were best friends.

The World was watching as the 9 Astronauts and 6 AI Robots all went into the Starship. Nancy and Kate were so proud of John while they were watching everything on TV at the hospital with a bunch of doctors and nurses.

John gave the count down and then it lifted off without a sound since magnets were used to get it into space. Again, everyone in the world was amazed.

Once they were out of the Earth's atmosphere, they set the coordinates for Mars and started up the Black Hole Propulsion system and the Starship reached Mars within the day. Once they reached Mars, they deployed the Space Station and AI Robot to the surface of Mars.

Everything had gone as planned and the AI Robot was doing various tests on the Mars surface and already expanding the Space Station and started using the Mars Rover. They all stayed there one day to make sure everything was going well and then John gave the command to come home and leave the AI Robot on Mars to continue its work.

As the Mars Starship landed, there were 3 other Starship waiting to take off to make sure that everything went well on the Mars trip. It was amazing to see the Mars Starship land and the other 3 Starships ready to take off.

Since the trip to Mars went well. All the AI Robots performed well, everyone thought that they should be able to do this next trip just using AI Robots.

There were some unknowns during the voyage that only AI Robot had to be deployed and can identify. The central computer which communicates with the AI Robots learned a great deal on the trip to Mars. These same AI Robot would be used on the next trip.

The AI Robots will have to be able to perform basic human tasks like working at a bank, opening bank accounts for new customers and talking about credit cards and interest. They also have to be used to talking with customers and solving their problems. The AI Robots that would be on the Starships have to be good at something besides flying the Starships. Russia, United States and China all will be using the same AI Robots, and each was building black hole starships. For this mission, all three countries will fly the black hole starships to Sirius and Proxima Centari.

They will go to places that are not too far and are not hostile, since they believe there could be human beings like us that live out there. These two places are in a section of the Milky Way galaxy called the Orion spur which runs perpendicular to the second and third spiral arm and joining the two arms.

Earth is located in the Orion spur closest to the second spiral arm and Sirius is farther out in the Orion spur and so is Proxima Centari. Starships are really called superluminal because they go faster than light. These superluminal ships from all three countries will fly together there with the AI Robots and the three black hole starships engines. The three starships from three countries are flying together for a three-month mission to Sirius and to Proxima Centari. They are to observe the centurions on Proxima Centari and also the Sirians from Sirius. We want the AI Robots to get all the data from the trips and to give it to all of the three countries involved and the world. All 3 Starship will be taking off from the US since they will be using the magnets to get out of the Earth's atmosphere.

Everyone in the World were amazed to see the 3 Starship takeoff together and then once out of the Earth's atmosphere engage their Black Hole Propulsion system go together as they trudge deeper into the space.

They left on their mission and the Starships passed by Alpha Centari first where there were extremely dangerous aliens that they saw but the AI Robots performed flawlessly on their mission and flew right pass them onto their next mission towards Proxima Centari.

They got to observe Proxima Centari and saw ships flying around them and observing them, but no problems have been identified by the AI Robots or the three starships. Then they left there and went to Sirius and observed ships taking off and landing from Sirius and some people in ships coming right by the AI Robots Starship, but they were successful in staying on their mission to observe, and the AI robots did that, and then they returned to earth three months later with no damage to the three starships.

During those 3 months, Kate had another surgery to take the bag off since her colon was healed. Kate was a little weak from the 2 surgeries, but all the cancer was gone. Kate had to stay in the hospital for a few days so she would have to watch everything from the hospital.

As the people around the World were watching all 3 Starships land together in the US space stations, they then extracted each starship's data from the trip and were evaluated so they would be ready when humans endeavor to go on a similar space mission.

A press conference was scheduled for Monday. The data gathered needed to be evaluated and it was Sunday, so John and Kate went to Church and then had a dinner planned at the Presidents dining room with the Space leaders from Russia, China, Switzerland, South Korea and the US. The Presidents of each of the countries were invited via zoom.

The AI Robots that were on the Starships were also invited in case there were questions about the data collected. These AI Robots were amazing. You could ask them a question and most of the time they would be able to give you the correct answer.

You need to learn how to converse with an AI robot in a meeting. At the beginning of the meeting, you need to let the AI Robot not talk but just listen or they will respond to every question in the meeting. You need to let them know you will ask them a question but not to interrupt conversation.

John remembers the first time he saw an AI robot and it was in an operating room. The Medical school was training new surgeons and John walked into the room. When John walked into the room he was talking to a doctor and all of a sudden, the AI robot that was laying on the operating table started answering John's questions. The doctor John was talking to had to tell the AI Robot to be quiet.

The AI robot on the operating table did not speak again until the doctor told him to speak. That particular AI robot that trained new doctor cost $250,000. These AI robots that were on the Starships were even more sophisticated and cost 1 million dollars.

The meeting in the President's dining room was unusual because it consists of the Space leaders from Russia, China, Switzerland, South Korea, Japan, the United States and John and Kate. Also in attendance were 6 AI Robots, 2 AI Robots each from Russia, China and US Starships. In addition, there were 5 Presidents, and 1 Prime Ministers All were on zoom except the US President.

The whole trip went as planned. This is why everyone loved John and Kate. Their design and testing of the AI robots and Starships were perfect.

Therefore, the questions were focused on humanoids and other

Space craft. It looks like they were observing, and we were observing. They were already talking about the next trip with Human Astronauts for a possibility to open up communications with the Aliens.

They all decided to conduct a Worldwide Press Conference by 9am US time so it can be shown live in Russia and China. The same people that were in this meeting would also be the same people at the Press Conference.

When the meeting was over, John went back to the hospital and when he entered Kate's room it was full of doctors and nurses watching the TV and they let out a loud cheer when John walked in. John could see that Kate was feeling better. They said she could be discharged on Sunday.

The Worldwide Press Conference

John and Kate woke up at 6:00am and John got into his exercise and decided to run to the gym and have some breakfast at the diner. To his surprise Katelin and Kate decided to join him. They took the limo to the diner though since Kate could not run as of yet.

John always liked to be with his beautiful wife and daughter. They have been eating together since Katelin was born. Now she was 30 and being the youngest person on the board of her company and his wife was known all over the World. John knew he was the luckiest man alive.

They talked about the Press Conference, but mostly about what was happening with Katelin. They kept giving her bigger and bigger assignments. They were now talking to her about running a separate part of the business that they were going to spin off where she would have a research, development, test, maintenance, marketing and sales group reporting departments reporting to her. She would be the President of that spin off company.

As John thought about Katelin, he would see a beautiful little girl, having a few more curves than her skinny girlfriends. Kate would keep her into swimming and sports, so she remained competitive and so as not gain weight. Katelin was so competitive; Kate took her out of swimming because she was getting muscles in her shoulders and arms. It was amazing how Kate would develop Katelin mentally and physically without Katelin knowing. It was fun for Katelin, and she always did what her mother told her to do.

Then when she turned 16 and moved to Tokyo, she became more beautiful and became a model. Kate could see this in Katelin and John thought he did not have a clue what was happening.

John remembered being on planes sitting next to other company executives and describing Katelin when she graduated from college and before he got off the plane the executives would hand John their card and ask him to have Katelin give them a call.

When John was alone, these thoughts would come back to him. As John sat across from Katelin, she would always be his little girl. Now he would brag about her to everyone.

Now she was a step ahead of most people. He remembered her telling Kate when Kate was going to the hospital. 'Don't worry about Daddy, I will take care of him if anything bad happens to you.'

Kate then looked at John with a serious stare and said, "John, are you okay? It looks like you were daydreaming. We need to get going or we will be late to our own Press Conference."

John with a little smile said, "I guess I was daydreaming, but it was a good dream. I am ready."

John got up and ran home and got ready to go to work with Kate. When they got to their office Jim and the President were waiting for them. They were surprised to see Kate, but Kate assured them that she is completely well and healed and doesn't want to miss the press conference. They reviewed everything they were going to say at the Press Conference and how everything would flow and then, before they all walked into the Press Conference. John pushed Kate up to the door of the Press Conference and then Kate opened the door and walked in. Kate could walk short distances, so John wheeled her to the press conference and then she walked all the way inside.

As the Space Leaders from Russia, China, Switzerland, South Korea, Japan, the United States and John and Kate walked into the room the TVs were turned on with the 4 other Presidents and the Prime Minister were all visible via zoom. The 6 AI robots were already seated on the stage. As they were walking towards the stage there was applause from everyone in the room. The standing applause did not stop until the US President got up and said, "My fellow leaders on Zoom, especially myself and the entire world are very proud of all of these people and the AI Robots. A lot of great things happen and also there is more to come in the future, so let me call John and Kate to give you all an update on the mission that just happened and what will happen."

As John and Kate approached the Podium there was applause and even the other Presidents and Prime Minister and their staffs on camera were applauding. John and Kate were known to everyone around the world, and they were both well- respected and loved.

Kate spoke first and introduced each Space leader and asked them to say a few words about what they did on the trip. So, the Space Leader from Switzerland talked about the particle collider and how the black holes were made. Then he went on and talked about the future using two black holes boxes spinning around making two gravity forces work together. Then she had Japan and South Korea talk about the making of the AI Robots. Then she had the Russian, Chinese and US Leaders get up and talk about how they made the Spaceships.

Everyone received applause when they got up to speak. Then Kate got each of the Presidents and Prime Ministers to say something about the Project. After each of the Leader spoke, they also received applause.

Then Kate introduced John to talk about what happened on the mission and the future missions. When Kate finished and John got up there was more applause. Kate then sat down. When John got up, he wanted to let everyone know how The Medical computer helped them pick the right doctor for Kate and also the surgery she just had, but did not want to take away anything that happen on the Space Project so John said in a very serious tone, "As everyone knows since this mission was the first of its kind, we decided to send our best AI robots. Everything on the mission went as planned and it was a great success.

During the mission we took the following photos and videos.

A video came on the screen and was fed Live around the World. As the movies and photos were being shown, John said, "We showed these to the Presidents, Prime Minister and staff we all decided that we will need to make a return trip with AI Robots and Human Astronauts from our countries. As you can see there were other spacecraft circling the 3 Starships.

They attempted to communicate with us, and we attempted to communicate with them in different languages and signs. We are evaluating their communications and from what we can translate, they want to meet with us face to face. They asked us to land now or come back sometime and land.

Our Presidents and Prime Minister have all agreed to go back in one month with Human Astronauts. We told them in one of our communications we would try to come back. They seem friendly and I believe they know we are friendly too.

One month will give us enough time to try to understand their language so we can communicate with them. We will see if we can improve it on the Starship. So, we will have another Press Conference in one week to give you an update. This is very exciting, and we look forward to meeting these identities from outer space."

When John finished his talk, everyone stood up and applauded. You can also hear cheers from the press people that joined on Zoom.

John, Kate and everyone on stage including the AI robots left the stage and went to John and Kate's conference room for a quick huddle. When they left the conference room, Kate sat down in her wheelchair and John pushed her to the conference room. When they got to the conference room, they could still hear the cheering. Kate stood up and said," This was a great day. There will be more surprises coming up. We will all be very busy with the Space Project and some new projects we will bring forward.

I know that all of you know I had my cancer removed from my colon and we did not want to talk about that at the Press Conference. I want everyone to know if it wasn't for The Medical Project computer I would not be here today. We used that computer to find my surgeon and he was able to perform a surgery that no other doctor could do. I owe the medical computer my life. If anyone here ever gets sick, please use the computer we have developed.

I will be fully recovered by the next Press Conference in one month and we will be talking about your next projects and also the Space project. Everyone will have to wait one month, and we will show them the next chapter. For now, John will be helping with my recovery for a couple of weeks."

The President, all the leaders, Jim and Jim's wife Nancy, were in the conference room. They all stood up and cheered and Nancy gave John and Kate a big hug. She knew what they both went through a lot, since she spent many nights with them at the hospital sleeping on a couch in Kate's room while John was sleeping in a chair. They were her best friends forever.

Everyone stood up and cheered for John and Kate and started a chant saying, "We will see you in one month."

After so many successes and challenges, John and Kate Columbo became legends and heroes in their own rights and people remembered them for their great contribution and will always remember them as the power couple that helped save the world.

-END-